Entry into Gwerinatha

"Wow!" exclaimed Cameron Gray as he walked through the portal as it began to close. "Did you see these weird trees, Bobby? Bobby?" Cameron turned around to discover that he was no longer within shouting distance of his friend Robert Moore. In fact he was just about to realize that he had no idea at all where he was or how he could possibly return home. "What the—? Hey Bobby! This isn't a funny joke. Where are you?" Cameron looked around in vain, spinning in circles and holding the portal key up to the sun at every possible angle hoping for some miraculous reappearance of the doorway. He stood still for a moment and lowered the key. "Crap!"

A beleaguered look came over his face. His shoulders dropped. He took a deep breath and let out a tremendous sigh. He breathed in again and then out again. "Whoa!" he exclaimed. "The air here is different. It feels like I'm breathing for the first time!" His sense of dread quickly disappeared and he started to look around. Rolling green hills dotted with small bushes surrounded him. The sky was a bright blue and the sun shone down brightly giving Cameron a clear view of his new surroundings. Seeing nothing but meadows he decided to roam about.

He walked slowly at first, carefully taking in all the scenery such as it was. Though the area seemed rather disinteresting to his mind it was new to him all the same and thus demanded his attention. Before he knew it his pace had picked up and it wasn't long before he had traveled quite a distance from where he had started. After about an hour of wandering around the meadows it had started to sink in that he was stranded in a new and different world. "What am I gonna do here?" he asked himself. "There is *nothing* here. Miles and miles of nothing. I don't understand. Bobby walked in, disappeared for only a couple of seconds and then walked right back out. How did he do it? Why did I have to go and jump in head first without thinking? Now the blasted doorway has closed and I'm stuck here in Nowheresville."

The Legend of Gwerinatha
Chaos' Corner

by Brad Parnell

A BlackWyrm Book
Louisville, Kentucky

THE LEGEND OF GWERINATHA: CHAOS' CORNER

Copyright ©2011 by BlackWyrm

A BlackWyrm Book
BlackWyrm Publishing
10307 Chimney Ridge Ct, Louisville, KY 40299

Printed in the United States of America.

ISBN: 978-1-61318-111-9
LCCN: 2011932195

Cover by Brad Parnell
Interior Illustrations by Brad Parnell
Edited by Kate Chawansky

First edition: July 2011

DEDICATED TO:

My mother Jessie,
who appreciated and encouraged
all my creative endeavors from the very beginning.

Our complicated cat Max,
who had a tragic beginning and ending
but who turned into a wonderful friend in the meantime.
He was inspirational to this part of the legend.

Special thanks again to Dave, Jason, and Simon.

Preface

The Originators of Gwerinatha had never counted on human intrusion. Familiar with human beings in general they had planned on their creation to be free of them. The day Samuel More brought six couplings of humans with him into their world changed that forever. The humans stirred a brew of controversy within the Originators. Numbering seven in total, the Originators' opinions on the new inhabitants were quite varied. There was the opinion that they deserved to live side by side comfortably with the Originators' creation. There was also the opinion that they should be forced to go back from whence they came. Many generations went by with the humans continuing to multiply. Something had to be done. The fact remains that the only compromise that could be reached was to abandon the project completely and start anew elsewhere. This decision was not met with enthusiasm by all members and one in particular was more than displeased.

Chapter 1
Let There Be Light

The Unfinished Lands were unusually still and quiet on this particular morning. Deep in the heart of the long abandoned city, the palace of the Originators stood tall above all else. Despite the chaos that surrounded the edifice, it had always stayed the same. It remained unmoved by the land around it which would crumble apart, gather back together, and crumble again. The lightning which only appeared in this one area of Gwerinatha never struck it. Waves of water which came from flash floods never even got it wet. Earthquakes, fires, mobs of marauding monsters and many other common violent occurrences in the Unfinished Lands left it unharmed. Inside the palace there had been darkness for uncounted years until this uncommonly still and quiet morning.

From outside the palace on the hills to the north it could be seen. Just a small light at first, it lit up one window in the interior of the palace. Then with a pattern of symmetry unseen in the Unfinished Lands it lit all the windows in the palace from the center outwards until the entire palace shone like a beacon. Then as quickly as it came it dimmed. The light did not go out completely. From those northern hills the light could still be seen in several of the windows. No longer did it appear as if the palace was lifeless.

Someone was home.

From various locations in the Unfinished Lands came huge creatures that seemed to be beckoned by the light as if it were some sort of signal. One by one they crawled, crept and slithered into the palace. The invitation to the housewarming had gone out and the guests were arriving. Slowly they filled the main hall until there was very little room for anyone else.

The main hall of the palace was quite large and had room enough for a few score of their number. It was decorated with light colors and elegant ornaments. It looked as though it could have been used as a place of worship. Despite the time that had passed since the original occupants had been gone it looked as if no one had ever left. There was neither dust nor cobwebs to be seen anywhere. The floors shone as if they had just recently been waxed. The walls were pristine as if no one had ever touched them after they'd been erected. This was a place that had clearly not been intended for the visitors that were now sauntering about and tracking the dirt in from beyond the walls.

The creatures in the main hall were quite different from the humans that inhabited the rest of Gwerinatha. They were an odd assortment of descendants from the original unfinished creatures and the cursed humans from centuries ago. They were tall, short, thin, stout, old and young. Some appeared to have the strength to rip a large tree out of the ground. Others looked like they would break in two if they encountered a heavy breeze. Still each one of them had an ominous visage. A considerable variety showed in their gene pools. Some looked like bizarre amalgamations of humans and wild animals. Others looked like rejected misfits of malicious genetic experiments gone awry. The one thing they had in common regarding their appearance was that they were all quite hideous to the human eye.

As the last of their kind came into the main hall a buzz filled the air. It wasn't clear if they knew just why they had gathered here. None of them could keep perfectly still though they didn't have much room to move about. Some of them just stood in place and moved subtly back and forth with their upper bodies. Others seemed to be slightly agitated and would hop up and down. Still others would twist around in circles looking about as if to see if everyone had arrived. For the most part they were all relatively silent. If any of them could speak, they were holding their tongues. A few gurgles and mumbles could be heard but not so much as to be a major distraction.

Then the earliest arrivals that were in the front began to stiffen up. Like a wave sent throughout the crowd all the rest of the creatures that were moving became perfectly still. Those who had managed to make sounds were now perfectly silent. Something was about to happen. The reason they were all here would soon be apparent.

In the back of the great hall a light appeared. Small at first, it grew and grew until it was the size of the largest creature in the room; roughly three times that of an average man. The light was bright white and had no noticeable source. It floated around the room with no apparent pattern. After a few short moments it settled into the middle of the crowd as the creatures backed up to give it room. With all the creatures now in a large ring around the light it began to grow increasingly brighter. Soon every creature in the room that had limbs used them to shield their eyes from the blinding light. The rest clenched their eyes tightly or simply turned away. Then the entire palace went black in an instant and just as quickly the light returned to normal. Where the light once floated in the middle of the room a figure now stood.

Standing just over eight feet tall the figure towered over the largest creature in the room. It was dressed in a long flowing robe mainly colored yellow with gold trim. Its skin was pale and off-white with a yellow cast that could have been a reflection from the bright robe. It had no hair and large inset dark eyes that seemed to have no color at all. Tall and thin it moved about in a slow, graceful and deliberate manner.

"Welcome dear friends." the figure said. "I am Gule. You are all here because I have so commanded it. You will find that despite never having laid eyes upon me you will be compelled to do anything I ask of you, for I am one of a long gone group of beings who created this world and almost everything in it. My particular specialty was that of creating animal life and thus you are all descended in one way or another from my original creations."

Gule's voice was deep and almost threatening. His voice and mannerisms leaned towards that of a male in spite of his androgynous appearance. He looked around after a long pause and seemed almost perturbed by something.

"Some of you..." he continued, "...have been descended from a combination of my original creations and the accursed human interlopers who displeased us. I recall now how those men were cursed to live as beasts and I look around this room and can tell immediately which of you came from them." At this his look of displeasure was apparent. He seemed to look down his nose on some of the creatures at that moment. He went on, cocking his head to the left while his eyes looked to the right. "I tell you all that the humans are in reality the true beasts. But you... you are my children, even those of you unfortunate enough to have human blood in your veins. But you will all help me to finish the job my fellows and I began so many centuries ago. With you at my side we shall return Gwerinatha to its original purpose."

The crowd made its first sound since Gule's appearance. They roared and grunted with approval. Gule motioned to them to be silent and they hushed immediately. "How many of you are not fond of the human beings?" he asked. They roared and grunted again, this time much louder. "Good, good." Gule responded. "And how many of you would like to live in the rich lands that they have taken for themselves?" More grunts of approval followed. "I can *make* that happen. I want to *see* that happen. I want *my* children to have their rightful place in this world. The humans had their chance to leave after they first arrived. They refused and though my fellows could not agree on what appropriate action to take, I knew all along what should be done. They would not listen to me. They did not understand. Even as the years went on and the humans overtook the land and began spreading their sinful ways the others would not listen. Finally they realized only too late the damage the humans had done to our world. By then the only course of action agreed upon was to leave." He paused briefly and took a slow look around the room before continuing. "But now I have returned. And I am alone. What they say no longer matters for I am the only Originator in Gwerinatha. Mine is the only law and no one shall question it. Now I will finally enact what should have been done all those many years ago. Finally the humans will be eradicated from Gwerinatha and the damage they created can begin to be overturned."

His speech finished, he bade the creatures to take their leave until they were called upon again. All of them gradually filed out in the same orderly fashion in which they entered, all but one that is. After several minutes only one creature remained. His name was Granton. Granton was one of the oldest of those who dwelled in the Unfinished Lands. He stood about six feet tall and had skin as black as coal save for his grayish speckled birdlike legs. His arms were the most human like feature he possessed, something that was quite an advantage among his peers. His eyes were similar to Gule's in that they seemed colorless and were difficult to make out on his solid black face. His head was jagged and thick in a way that reminded you of a tree that had been struck by lightning. It was only when he spoke that you could see large yellow fangs inside his mouth. Granton was not an original creation of Gwerinatha but he did predate the cursed humans and their children. He walked in a stilted fashion towards Gule who stared at him in disbelief as he approached.

"I should like to stay, lord Gule." Granton hissed, his thick purple tongue getting caught up in his fangs. "I have waited a lifetime for your return and unlike the others I recognized you instantly. I feel more than they the sting of having my birthright taken from me. I should like to stay and be your personal assistant."

"At first I thought to admonish you for not leaving with the others." Gule responded. "But then I recognized you too. You were but a child, a child of two of my original creations, when I left Gwerinatha. How is it that you have come to live such a long life when no other creature here has matched your age?"

"That I cannot answer." replied Granton. "Save that my animosity for the humans has driven me onward."

"Yes." said Gule. "You could be of assistance to me. Very few of the others can speak at all thanks in part to the humans' interference. It will be nice to have someone that can carry on a conversation here with me. The other Originators shall not be coming back and it is possible that within the allotted time I have here that I could benefit from some companionship." He raised his hand and swept it towards Granton as a gracious gesture. "Very well, you shall be my personal assistant and you can begin by helping me set up what I will call... our war room."

Near the top floor of the palace there was a large room with seven thrones. It was here the Originators would plan the creation of Gwerinatha and it was here that Gule and Granton began setting up their war room. They set up a large map of the world with markers indicating where the human villages and cities were located. And when Gule was satisfied with the layout of the room he walked up to the thrones and sat in the one located in the middle. "These others thrones will be unnecessary Granton." he said. "As I have said the others will not be coming back. Instead it is I who will have the sole decision in the fate of Gwerinatha unlike the last time I sat in this room."

Granton sat on the floor nearby listening intently to Gule as he described the last meeting of the Originators.

"They gave me no support Granton. None at all." he said, his anger building. "Oh there were those who agreed that the humans were trouble. Zold for example, she who controlled the very ground this palace sits on. She knew that the humans were potentially harmful to the nature she so painstakingly crafted around us. And yet when it came to a vote she felt she could not do anything that would harm them. Harm *them* Granton! They were poison to the earth. They were causing us harm! Ridiculous! For a few years I did feel that Vermelho was of like mind. Originally he wanted the humans vanquished as I did. With his fiery nature I thought it only natural we could team up to go against the others and yet he changed his view to banishing the humans and eventually went along with the idea for us to start over instead. That was the idea of that blasted Horaens, sitting here in this middle throne lording over us as if he were a high king. Because his focus is the mind he believes himself to be our leader, ignoring the fact that we all speak for ourselves."

Gule then began to look disappointed as he looked at the empty thrones and then over to Granton. "What is the matter?" asked Granton. "You seem disturbed."

"I was just thinking about the others." Gule responded. Without their assistance I will not be able to create any life in a permanent fashion."

"What do you mean?" inquired Granton.

"We will need an army Granton." began Gule's answer. "Some of the creatures you saw here today are fine for the art of war but many others are not. We will need more help. My role was to create bodies. Mine is the strength of the physical nature. I created the animals..." his voice trailed off as his thoughts obviously went back to another time. "It was my finest creation, the one I was most proud of that these humans had the gall to destroy!" Gule's white face began to darken, the yellow tint going from orange to red. "The thing is what to do without the others. You see, Zold created the plants and the rest of the nature. We all worked together and we cannot work independently of one another to create anything with permanence. You see I made the bodies but without Anil's touch to allow them to breathe her air or Mavi's touch to give them his life giving water, my creation may not last long. Not to mention what one of my creations may be without Vold giving them a spirit to direct them. I still have plenty of power you see, but any creature I devise without the others will only live to do my bidding a short while. We must consider this heavily when planning our attacks against the humans. I may need something else to give me an advantage. Something I have yet to consider."

Chapter 2
Here We Go Again

"Wow!" exclaimed Cameron Gray as he walked through the portal as it began to close. "Did you see these weird trees, Bobby? Bobby?" Cameron turned around to discover that he was no longer within shouting distance of his friend Robert Moore. In fact he was just about to realize that he had no idea at all where he was or how he could possibly return home. "What the—? Hey Bobby! This isn't a funny joke. Where are you?" Cameron looked around in vain, spinning in circles and holding the portal key up to the sun at every possible angle hoping for some miraculous reappearance of the doorway. He stood still for a moment and lowered the key. "Crap!"

A beleaguered look came over his face. His shoulders dropped. He took a deep breath and let out a tremendous sigh. He breathed in again and then out again. "Whoa!" he exclaimed. "The air here is different. It feels like I'm breathing for the first time!" His sense of dread quickly disappeared and he started to look around. Rolling green hills dotted with small bushes surrounded him. The sky was a bright blue and the sun shone down brightly giving Cameron a clear view of his new surroundings. Seeing nothing but meadows he decided to roam about.

He walked slowly at first, carefully taking in all the scenery such as it was. Though the area seemed rather disinteresting to his mind it was new to him all the same and thus demanded his attention. Before he knew it his pace had picked up and it wasn't long before he had traveled quite a distance from where he had started. After about an hour of wandering around the meadows it had started to sink in that he was stranded in a new and different world. "What am I gonna do here?" he asked himself. "There is *nothing* here. Miles and miles of nothing. I don't understand. Bobby walked in, disappeared for only a couple of seconds and then walked right back out. How did he do it? Why did I have to go and jump in head first without thinking? Now the blasted doorway has closed and I'm stuck here in Nowheresville."

He walked up to the highest elevation he could see, that being a rather large hill, and took in a scan of the area all around him. He then sat down on the side of the hill and began to pick grass. With no sense of urgency he began to throw the blades of grass into the air one by one until he noticed something odd. At first he thought his eyes were playing tricks on him but then he stared a little harder and realized that there were plants that were vibrating a few yards away from his feet. He bolted up and ran over to them. These were Molerarods, bright red plants with spongy flowers that excrete gelatinous ooze some find quite tasty. Cameron stood directly over them as the plants' vibrations began to increase. As he leaned in to more closely examine one of them it sprayed him with its golden fruity pollen. "Waugh!" yelled Cameron. "What *is* this stuff? Hey, it tastes good!" he said as he licked it off his face. "Yeah, this stuff is pretty good." He noticed that each plant's vibrations would increase just before spewing forth this newly discovered snack. He went from plant to plant taking in as much as he could until he had his fill. He noticed that some of the plants had variations in the colors of their secretions. With each color came a slightly different flavor, all very sweet. Wiping his mouth he sat back against the hillside and looked up at the sky. "This place might not be so bad after all." he thought.

Just then what looked like a rotted red log in the distance stood up, sprouted legs and ran off. "Whoa, that was weird." thought Cameron. "Was that red log was alive? Nah! Couldn't be! But I'm sure I saw legs on it. That's got to be my eyes playing tricks on me. But I'm sure there was a log there and now it's gone. Maybe that was some kind of animal, like a turtle? I wonder what other kind of weird animals live around here?"

Cameron stood up and walked back to the top of another large hill. He gazed around more intently this time and after spotting a forest in the distance, he got it into his head that there may be even more wildlife to discover deep within. He set forth into the woods known as Anhysbys Forest. Cameron looked for any kind of life he could see. There was to him no noticeable trace of animals around. All he could see were trees, vines, bushes, rocks and lots of dirt covered with moss, twigs and dead leaves. He began to rethink his plan but as he kept going he realized there was something about the forest that made him feel comfortable. He had never spent too much time in the outdoors when he was home. He had been camping once or twice and had one summer away at a camp near a lake but he never considered himself the outdoors type. But he never actually hated or feared the outdoors either. He used to laugh at the nerdy kids in camp who were scared and would tease them about poison oak or torment them with stories of oversized wasps and mosquitoes. A grin came to his face as he reminisced about their reactions. Before he knew it he had walked for miles and finally decided it would be a good idea to sit and rest. He found a cozy looking spot against a very large tree. There he sat down and though he fought it for a while, he began to nod off.

Minutes went by as Cameron Gray slept peacefully. His calm nap was abruptly halted by a stabbing pain in his stomach. "Ow!" he exclaimed. "What's goin' on?"

He opened his eyes to see a rather large monkey, comparatively speaking, poking at his stomach with a broken off tree branch. The monkey jumped back and dropped the branch, startled by Cameron's outburst. "What are you doing?" Cameron screamed. "Oh man, that's a huge monkey! What, are you like seven feet tall?"

"Actually I am six feet and seven inches from tip to tail if you must know." the monkey replied.

"Aggh!!" Cameron screamed. "You can talk!"

The monkey jumped up into the tree at Cameron's second out burst causing the branches to shake violently. "You've got to stop doing that." the monkey exclaimed. "You are working on my nerves!"

"B-but, but," Cameron eked out. "You can talk." he repeated quietly almost as if to himself.

"We have established that human. I can talk. I can talk. I can talk." the monkey said with a frustrated tone. "You can talk. The squirrels can talk. All God's children can talk. But frankly I get the feeling *you* aren't a brilliant conversationalist."

"What?" Cameron retorted.

"My point exactly." the monkey said smugly. "Despite my curiosity, stirred by your strange clothes you are beginning to bore me. Now that I know you are not dead and not likely to harm me I shall take my leave." With that, the monkey climbed up high into the trees and the forest canopy began to shake with his weight as he swung from branch to branch and tree to tree until he was soon completely out of hearing distance.

"That was a t-talking m-monkey." Cameron said, barely getting the words out of his mouth. He stood up slowly shivering with fright just a little. He looked all around without moving his feet and then walked slowly around the tree he had been napping against. He then stood still and without moving his head he moved his eyes back and forth until he was sure there was nothing else to see. "I must be imagining things!" he yelled as he threw his face into his hands. "No!" he yelled again. "This can't be! But I am in a strange place. I did walk through that portal. What the heck is this place? How do I get out of here?"

Chapter 3
Can't We All Just Get Along

"How did I get myself into such a mess?" asked Samuel pouring through a pile of papers set in front of him on a large ornate desk. The office Samuel sat in was in the heart of New London where he had been residing most of his waking hours since returning from his self imposed exile. "This is utter madness. What have you people been doing to each other in my absence? Have you no sense of decency? Have you no brotherly love?"

"I'm not sure I understand your meaning." Governor Baileys replied standing behind Samuel with a frustrated look on his face. "This is how we've done things since long before I took office."

"That's just it!" moaned Samuel. "This has gone on for far too long. It has to stop."

"What has to stop?" asked the Governor.

"This constant bickering between the House of Fates and the Lords of Wisdom." Samuel took a breath as he looked around the cluttered room that resembled a lawyer's office with its many shelves filled to the ceiling with thick books. "It saddens me that you can't see any of this right in front of your face. I've poured over notes I have taken from my interviews these last several days. It seems that years ago the House of Fates actually had more power than they do now. There were many scandals that went on including bribery as well as rather intimate affairs I am too embarrassed to discuss and those in charge just covered them up as if they didn't happen."

"Yes, yes. See what I mean? Those people are shameless!" interrupted the governor. "Absolutely shameless!" The governor nodded his head back and forth with a scowl.

"Do not be so quick with your judgment Padrig." Samuel came back. "Since the Lords of Wisdom gained control they too have been involved with far too similar scandalous activity that has also gone unpunished." Samuel stared at Padrig intently before continuing. "I don't think I seem to be getting through to you. You asked me to be your advisor, a role I took on with a begrudging sense of duty, but it is a role I have taken very seriously. I would hope that you take to heart each thing I have to say to you Padrig. The very soul of Gwerinatha is at stake. "

"Oh I have been listening Samuel. I have." retorted Padrig trying a little too hard to be believable.

"Listen, Padrig." Samuel went on, "You must be more serious about opening dialogue with the south. I have been on the job a few weeks now and although everyone seemed optimistic about change and unity at first, it seems we have already taken a huge step backwards. Twice now meetings between you and the leaders of the House of Fates have been postponed." Samuel leaned back and cocked his head to the side and gave a quizzical look to Padrig. "I have come under the belief that you are putting these talks off out of a sense of fear."

"That's ridiculous." Padrig blurted out with a huff. "I've just been very busy you know. Expectations have been heightened with your reappearance. There have been so many new issues to address..."

"Deer feathers Padrig!" exclaimed Samuel. "My arrival and new position have not put you out so much that you cannot set and keep a date for what may prove to be the most important meeting in your political career. I have listened to your other excuses and frankly I am growing most weary."

"But Samuel," Padrig burst, "these people are intolerant buffoons! They never use their minds. They insist on letting fate decree everything for them. They will not listen to reason and act insufferably superior to us because we do not think the way they do. It is impossible to create a dialogue with such as these!"

"What do they wish for their people?" asked Samuel in a reserved tone.

"What?" replied Padrig. "What do you mean?"

"What I mean to say," continued Samuel, "is that if you'd thought to stop and consider what they wish for their people you may realize that you are not so very different at the core." Padrig rubbed his brow and slumped into his chair while Samuel pressed on. "You know I have visited the south and I have had some discussion with loyalists to the House of Fates. I know they want their people to be well fed. I believe they want their farms to flourish. I am certain they want to be able to sleep at night and not have to worry about savage beasts attacking or going to war with their fellow Gwerinathans. These are all things that everyone here in the north care about as well Padrig, are they not? It would appear they have all the same base dreams and fears as everyone around you here in New London. They just have a different way of going about it."

"That's all well and fine Samuel but they also want a lot of things that we in the Lords of Wisdom cannot tolerate."

"There you go again Padrig. You are only concerned with the differences. Yes, yes there are differences with the way you think and act but you have got to start concentrating on the similarities if you ever want to get anywhere with the unity movement."

Padrig's eyes began to drift off as he sunk his chin into his thumb and forefinger. He sat quietly for a moment as if he'd given up the argument with Samuel; his eyes going back and forth between disappointment and resentment.

"You are interested in the unity movement are you not Padrig? Because if you are only going along with me as some sort of ruse just so you can keep power I shall become greatly discouraged and take my opinions to the people."

"No! No!" Padrig pleaded as he jumped out of his chair. "You have got me all wrong Samuel. I believe in uniting Gwerinatha and I still have hopes that it can be done. I just lost my head for a moment there. Old habits die hard you know? I'll get that meeting with the Lords of the House of Fate rescheduled right away."

"...and?" Samuel said with a glare that stabbed deep into the Governor's face.

"...and I will promise to keep it." finished Padrig. "Nothing in all the Unfinished Lands could cause me to break the next appointment."

Chapter 4
Back to the Garden

"Are we there yet?" Charity Baylies asked her older sister Seren for what seemed to her like the thirtieth time in the last twenty minutes.

"Just a little further Charity." Seren replied. "We just have to make it past a few more of these large trees and it'll be in the next clearing. You're making me regret my decision to let you tag along."

"Aw, frits and weezles Ser, you know I'm old enough now." replied Charity.

"You're nowhere near old enough to come here without your elders." Seren retorted. "This trip was meant for me to show Mercy and Grace how to tend Branwen's garden now that they're old enough."

"Right Seren," said Mercy. "This was to be our day here now that we've turned thirteen and all. We're almost as old as Seren was when she first came here."

"The only reason you're here is because you put up such a fuss that you can't be shut up." Grace added.

"I'm only a year younger than you two you know." quipped Charity.

"Again," Grace repeated, "you can't be shut up."

"And you're a year and a *half* younger than us." added Mercy.

Charity rolled her eyes and became quiet for the first time in a long while if only out of spite. The girls had been walking most of the morning since being let out of a carriage near the edge of the forest. They walked a little further before finally entering into the clearing that was near Branwen's garden. They had come equipped with spades and seeds of various types of flowers to begin a new planting season for the garden. The clearing was empty. Once it was home to Arthur's wolf pack but since Branwen's death the area had gotten too much human traffic for their liking and thus they moved elsewhere. Most of the humans were Branwen's friends or family paying their respects. Other human visitors were wildlife defenders who thought of the place as a sort of shrine to their movement. The area was too far out of the way to become a tourist attraction and with that and the fact Serenity Forest was still considered dangerous by most of the populous, the human traffic was relatively light. Even still it had become too uncomfortable for Arthur's tastes. He had decided to move the family elsewhere to keep them safe. The wolves did still visit on occasion however.

"There it is girls," Seren said, pointing towards the garden. "Our sister's legacy. It's up to us to keep it looking good."

The girls sorted out their gardening tools on the ground as Seren showed them around. She pointed out where the flowers were to go and which vegetables to plant where. With the wolves gone the original intent for the garden had vanished with them. Now however, Seren, her sisters and the wildlife defenders thought of the garden as a symbol for all that Branwen represented. It reminded them of her devotion to the animals and with the debate still raging about hunting in Serenity Forest it gave them a focal point to rally around.

Seren stood over her sisters as they worked. A smile crept across her face as she watched them. Initially she intended for the twins to start helping her with this task without their youngest sister but it seemed Charity was every bit as eager as her older sisters, possibly even more so. She didn't need as much direction as Seren had thought either. But then Charity had always played around in the gardens back in their home in Baylies Crossing. Seren had thought that was all she did but it seems she had learned quite a bit by watching the gardeners there. She seemed more at ease in the dirt than Mercy and Grace. But she still wondered if Charity was mature enough to handle the sometimes frightening forest surroundings.

As Charity dug earnestly into the dirt her twin sisters stopped to wipe their brows. Being identical twins doing things at the same time wasn't all that unusual for them. When they were about to begin digging again they noticed a second shadow next to Seren's that wasn't there before. It started growing ever so gradually. Both twins turned simultaneously to see the source of the mysterious shadow and when they did they let out a huge scream.

The scream caused Charity to look up from her work and when she saw the shadow's source she joined them in their still continuing screams. At the same time Seren bolted around to see a wolf lunging toward her. She instinctively raised her hands in a defensive measure but then quickly moved them outward in order to embrace the wolf now mere inches from her chest.

"Louie!" yelled Seren. "It's so good to see you. Where have you been?"

"We have a new home now Seren." replied Louie now in a tight hug. "I've been there with the rest of the pack when I haven't been starting new adventures. Are these your sisters?"

"Yes." answered Seren. "The two cowering together on the ground over there are Mercy and Grace and the little one who was about to stab you with a spade is Charity."

Charity had gotten up and moved towards them with the spade clutched in her hand like a spear. Once she realized no harm was coming to them she lowered it and became embarrassed.

"Don't worry." said Louie. "It's not a bad idea to always be prepared for battle in the woods. You never know what crazed monster might be lurking in the bushes. I shouldn't have jumped like that but I couldn't resist surprising Seren."

The twins now standing but still huddled close together began looking around to see if some other not-so-friendly creatures might be lurking about nearby.

"It's okay girls." Seren told them. "He was only *sort* of kidding. As long as we're here in the daylight and not alone we should be okay."

"Now that we've gone," added Louie, "the fiercest creatures in this part of the forest are the rabbits who eat all the food out of the garden."

"You've grown some in the few weeks since I've seen you last Louie."

"All the better to bring down deer. I'm big enough now that I can take down two all by myself and I'm not even fully grown yet."

"You'll be taking down whole herds in a month or two." said Seren.

Assured there were no other dangers, Mercy and Grace walked slowly over to meet Louie. Charity had already begun to pet him as if he was the family dog and he seemed to enjoy it. The twins then started petting Louie as well and he let out a little howl of contentment. Seren smiled even larger now. She knew Branwen would be quite pleased now that all her sisters were continuing her work and taking pleasure in knowing forest life as friends.

Chapter 5
Survival of the Fittest

As the weeks passed young Cameron Gray learned to become a survivor in the forest. His clothes became tattered and torn and in desperate need of a good washing but despite this he had become almost comfortable in his new situation. He first made meals of fruits and nuts he found along the forest floor. Then he learned where to find the trees and bushes that produced them. Later, he even started eating various bugs in hopes of gaining protein. Eventually he discovered the Didoriad River which runs straight through the middle of Anhysbys Forest. There he caught fish and gathered drinking water. He fancied himself as a wild jungle boy raised by animals and even began painting his face with colors he made from mud and berries. He fashioned hunting weapons out of rocks and branches and made meals of smallish rodents he was able to chase down before they were able to scamper back into their holes. He was quite thankful for his lighter which enabled him to easily start fires for cooking his meals. Although he had gotten in touch with his wilder nature he was still glad that not all of the animals he encountered could speak. He imagined he'd become more than a little unnerved by having a conversation with his dinner just before killing it.

For shelter he'd built himself a tree house of sorts. He found four very large trees that were situated in such a way that it was fairly easy to build a floor in between them several feet off of the ground. He made some makeshift tools out of rocks and sticks in much the same way he had made the weapons. A few large logs made nice handrails around the sides and a net of vines stretched in between the trees several feet below the canopy made a decent enough roof. Each day he would add more leaves on top of the vines for additional coverage. He found he could make a dye out of some of the berries and crushed flowers from some of the trees with which he made some paint for decoration. He painted the floor red and the handrails yellow. He mixed the two for some orange that he used to paint a name on one of the sides. He had thought of painting Robinson Crusoe there but couldn't remember how it was spelled so he settled on 'Cam's Place'. Once it was finished he stepped back and took it all in with a huge grin. All in all he was quite proud of his new abode.

At this point he had food and shelter, the maintenance of which took up the better part of his days. Still there seemed to him that there was something missing. It was something that he couldn't at first fully realize. Beyond the talking monkey he'd only thought he'd heard an animal speak maybe once or twice. It had gotten to the point that he believed he'd imagined the whole conversation. He was getting quite lonely. He yearned for any type of companionship. He would put the feelings out of his mind by concentrating on his tree house.

He had a hammock that he'd fashioned out of some more vines. Each night after he'd gotten enough food for the day he'd lie down in the hammock and stare up at his roof that was getting a little denser every day. He would listen as the trees would sing to him. He was sure that's what they were doing even though he had never heard any trees make noise like this from where he had originally come. It had to be singing. There was no other sound with which it compared. He even thought that if he tweaked the branches just right he could get different notes out of the trees as if he could possibly tune them. As he lay there, staring up and hearing the tree music each night it allowed him time to realize just how alone he actually was.

On a day much like so many of the others that had blurred by Cameron was out hunting for something to eat when he heard a strange noise. Not that most any noise in this new world wasn't strange to him but by now he'd gotten used to most of the forest sounds. This was different however. It sounded as if it were something moaning or shrieking. He couldn't be certain. He definitely heard the sound of leaves being shuffled. He looked around and considered the direction of the noise. As he silently crept toward the sound he began to crouch down and held out his homemade spear. Once he was close enough he was able to see what was making all the noise. A large beetle like creature was trying to take a small animal into its hole, presumably as dinner. This beetle was easily more than a foot long with long sharp mandibles that were like a bear trap. The creature struggling to get away was unlike anything Cameron had ever seen before. It walked on four legs although at the precise moment one of them was caught in the beetle's mandibles. It had a long tail and neck. Its head was small and round with tiny inset eyes. Cameron had a difficult time trying to figure out if it was a reptile or a mammal as it seemed to him to be a strange cross between the two. The whole thing was roughly the size of a small pig and had skin that was tough and leathery. Cameron's initial thought was to save the creature but he wasn't exactly sure why. As he watched it struggle he began to feel pity for it.

Cameron rushed out from behind a bush and screamed as he ran toward the creatures. His hope was that he could scare off the beetle into its hole and in so doing it would let go of the strange animal. Instead it held on even tighter as blood began to trickle down the caught beast's leg. The animal's moaning became louder as it was clear he was in a good bit of pain. His initial plan a failure, Cam kept running until he was close enough to stab at the beetle. The beetle's exoskeleton however was impenetrable at least as far as a sharpened branch was concerned and the force of the blow sent Cameron back on his heels.

With that, the beetle did let go of the beast and made a move toward Cameron. Just barely able to keep from falling, Cam steadied himself and braced for the beetle's attack. Just as it lunged for him he leapt over the beetle and turned sharply with his spear now held in the middle like a quarter staff. Before the beetle could get turned all the way around Cam started hammering at it back and forth with his spear knowing the blows wouldn't hurt it but hoping they'd at least get it to run off. The beetle kept snapping at the spear trying to break it. Cam was too quick with it however and kept bashing at it until it finally started moving backwards. It felt to Cam like a fencing duel in a way, his spear versus the sharp mandible of the beetle. If he could just keep the advantage long enough to get the beetle where he wanted him he'd be all right he felt. He had the beetle moving backwards in a circle. He kept maneuvering him until he was backed up near his hole. He had hoped to get the beetle to fall back into his hole but then with one particularly harsh whack of the spear he sent the beetle tripping backwards over a large rock in front of his hole and he caught it on its back. With no hesitation Cameron went in for the kill. He stabbed repeatedly at the soft inside of the beetle which gave little resistance after the second cut. He almost took glee in the fact that he had killed something that could have killed him. Unlike hunting this felt different to him. This wasn't killing for preservation. This was victory.

He stood for a moment leering over the dead beetle until the soft moans of the strange creature reminded him he was not alone. He turned his attention to the poor beast which was trying to limp away. The creature was definitely frightened and Cameron sensed this. "Hey there little fella, it's all right. Nobody's gonna hurt you." he said motioning to the animal with an open hand gesture. "The big bad beetle is dead now. Can you talk?" After a long pause with the animal just staring up at him Cam continued. "I guess not. What have you got there?" he said, reaching for his bleeding leg. "It looks like a pretty bad scratch. We can fix that. Let me take you back to my place and we'll have you up and on your way in no time."

After carefully moving towards it to make sure it wouldn't run off Cam slowly picked the little animal up. Its moans turned to a gurgle as Cam gently carried it back to his tree house. There he cleaned the wound and wrapped it in some leaves he thought were just right for bandages. He found the leaves to be similar to what he knew as an aloe plant back home. He had used them on himself after getting a little too close to the fire while cooking fish. He figured they would be soothing on a cut as well. The little creature seemed thankful and began to walk gingerly around Cameron's legs. Cam then reached down and picked him back up. "Here now," he told it. "I don't think we should be walking around just now. You sit here for a while." He placed him on a makeshift pillow of leaves in the corner of the tree house. The creature looked around for a while and then turned over on its side and went to sleep.

Cam stared at it for a while and then thought to himself, "Man that sure is an ugly little thing but I don't know... There's just something about it..." He decided that if the creature would like to stay he'd consider it a pet. He had no idea what it was, how big it would get or even if would remain friendly but for that night at least, he'd found himself a new friend.

Chapter 6
The Plan Begins

The throne room of the Originators was once a place of great wonder and excitement. The room had seven large thrones, one for each of the group. They were set up in a slight arc with one in the back on a step higher than the other six which were evenly balanced with three on either side. The thrones were all a deep red in color with a gold trim. The ornate decorations lining the thrones matched the decorations that appeared just above the moldings that went around the entire room. They used this place to gather and discuss the plans for the creation of Gwerinatha. This is where they would compare notes on how they would put the world together. After centuries of being abandoned by its creators the room was now being used to plot a restructuring of Gwerinatha. A new world order was being planned in which there was no place for humans. A room that was once full of joyful noise and light was now somber, sullen, and dim.

Gule sat on the main throne in a seeming daze, staring straight across the room at the large entryway doors. He had done this for several hours a day since returning to the palace. Sometimes he'd get a glimmer of an idea and begin to ponder it as if he'd found a solution to a puzzle. Then after mulling it over for a long while he'd let it go and search for another avenue. His trouble was twofold, first there was the large amount of humans which now lived in all the cities of Gwerinatha and second there was the inability to form an army that would last long enough to be particularly useful. Although he had great power as an Originator he couldn't just wipe the humans out in one fell swoop. It would take time and preparation and just the right method that could sate his thirst for vengeance. He would need to be especially careful in his military attacks on the villages with an army of temporary soldiers. He would need to use them in the right places at the right times or else he could face a backlash that would delay his goals. He didn't care so much for the lives of his creations. Neither did he fear for his own life. He knew he could vanish again if things got too difficult. But he also knew his time was limited and that he wouldn't be satisfied until each and every human in Gwerinatha was destroyed.

A knock came upon the door which was ignored at first. After a long pause Gule then turned from his deep thought to reply to the intrusive sound. "Yes?" he said moodily.

"It is I, Granton, my lord." came the voice from the other side of the door. "I bring news from the outside which may interest you." Granton knew not to bother Gule unless it was something he thought was really important. He also knew not to knock a second time as Gule could easily be perturbed. Granton was always on the good side of Gule but knew from watching him interact with other Unfinished Land inhabitants that he could be very erratic. He had seen him manifest creatures that would burrow around on the inside of the skin of anyone who had disturbed him and once even gave a creature an extra mouth that began to gnaw away at parts of his body.

"Come forward then Granton. Let's hear what you have to say."

Granton slowly opened the enormous doors and began walking toward Gule. It took him nearly a minute to make his way across the large room. His small legs had always had to work extra hard to carry around his weighty upper frame but at his advanced age it became even more difficult. Once he got to the foot of the throne he knelt down and addressed Gule. "There are reports of a strange human in Anhysbys Forest."

"Strange?" asked Gule. "In what way?"

"He is not at all like the others." replied Granton. "It seems he resembles an outsider from another world who recently visited here."

"Another world?" screamed Gule almost knocking Granton backwards. "What *other* world? Why was I not informed of a visitor from another world?"

"He returned to his home before you arrived lord Gule." answered Granton. "I had little knowledge of it myself until only recently."

"Go on." Gule grumbled.

"From my understanding the original visitor was instrumental in the extraction of Samuel More from the Unfinished Lands."

"Samuel? Still alive?!?" exclaimed Gule. "I am beginning to think I may need another assistant if it turns out you are keeping information from me Granton!"

"No, no my lord!" begged Granton. "I am getting information to you as quickly as I can. It has taken a while to piece this story together from the different citizens of the Unfinished Lands who have communicated with me. I know how important your solitude is and I want to make sure you have accurate information with which to destroy the humans."

"Yes, of course." he said with a satisfying tone. "We'll get back to Samuel later. His demise I may wish to witness personally. But what of this new stranger and why is it thought he came from another world?"

"Well his clothes were similar to that of the previous visitor I'm told." replied Granton. "Those who had captured him and his comrades also noticed similar mannerisms and speech patterns that are uncommon among the humans in the cities. This new stranger has been spotted fishing in the river and eating bugs and rodents in the forest. He seems to have had no contact with any of the humans to this point."

"Yes..." Gule said quietly. "You were right to bring this to my attention. This could be just what I need to... Bring him to me immediately!"

Yes, my lord. Right away..."

"No! Wait!" Gule interrupted. "I may have a better idea. Give me some time to think this through. Meanwhile ready some of the roughest looking citizens you can find. I'll need them to help me acquire this strange human."

Gule then went back to his pondering on the throne while Granton still kneeling waited to be addressed. "If I can turn one of their own against them," Gule thought aloud, "I could add confusion to the terror of my monstrous creatures. He could also be the leader my army needs as opposed to the undisciplined hordes which now surround me."

"But how can you make him turn against his fellow humans, lord Gule?" asked Granton.

"You said yourself he has yet to have human contact in this world, correct?"

"As far as we know this is true." answered the faithful assistant.

"Well then we shall have to make sure his only contact with them is that which we allow. After I have taken him under my wing and prepared him the day will come when he will gladly take our armies into battle to wipe out all the humans in Gwerinatha. And when his task is complete we will remove him and our goal will be accomplished." Gule then looked around the room and then down at Granton. He paused for a while as he considered strongly his next action. "This will take a great amount of time in preparation Granton. One such as I will have no problem with the patience required. I have waited centuries for this day. A few more years will be insignificant to me. You however may not last quite that long at your current state. I have just the thing. Come closer my servant."

Granton got up and walked the few steps in between the two of them. He then looked up at Gule. Gule reached down and put his hands on each of the gnarled shoulders of Granton. He then bowed his head and closed his eyes. A glow of energy began to emanate from within Gule. His body shifted from off white to bright yellow and the energy seemed to flow into Granton. Several minutes went by with no apparent change and then suddenly Granton began to shake violently and his craggy appearance began to smooth somewhat. His deeply set in sunken eyes seemed to brighten as his high cheeks shrunk down and softened. His tiny bird legs got a little thicker and stronger looking. His arms took on more tone and his skin lightened from coal black to a dark gray. Within an hour Gule had not only decreased Granton's age by a few centuries but increased his strength and mobility as well. When he was finished, Gule threw back his arms and Granton fell back onto the floor but was able to quickly get back to his feet.

Gule slumped back into the center throne and seemed to smile at Granton. "Thank you my lord." said Granton, in a less raspy, deeper voice. "This is a most glorious gift you have given me."

"It is but a small use of my power Granton." said Gule. "I wish the effects could be longer lasting but I think with a recharge here and there you should now be able to last until my plan has succeeded. I feel you deserve to witness my triumph as you have been through much in your longer than usual life span."

Gule then slowly sat up in the throne. He took a deep breath and thought for another moment before announcing his next command. "I shall go one step further Granton. Get that group of citizens together to go after this human as we have discussed. But do not have them bring him here. Have them take him to one of their own strongholds. There I will begin the next phase of my plan to take back Gwerinatha."

Chapter 7
Captured

Cameron woke up hungry. He had begun getting used to smaller meals than he had from home and his stomach had even begun to shrink somewhat. He wasn't used to eating breakfast at all but now with each meal getting harder to come by he would start the day off trying to find something to eat. He longed for the days when he could go to a fast food restaurant or grocery store and pick up what he wanted. He thought achingly about having a refrigerator to keep food at the ready. Even though he was adjusting to life in this strange new world, when it came to eating he missed home terribly. Cameron knew the hunger wasn't going to go away on its own so he started off in search of food. He looked over and noticed that his overnight guest had begun to stir as well.

"So. I guess you're hungry too." Cam addressed it. "What kind of stuff do you eat?" The creature just stared up at him tilting his head slightly and blinking his dark eyes which seemed to sparkle in the early morning sunlight. Cam reached over and rubbed its head. "Well I can tell from your teeth that you're no meat eater. So you can come with me I guess since I don't have much luck with finding meat anyway. Maybe you'll like some of the weird plants that I can eat." He then jumped down from the tree house and reached over for the little creature who had limped over to the edge. "Well now, it sure looks like you're walking a little better this morning. You should be good as new in no time." Cam picked him up and sat him gently on the ground. He then hobbled over to a nearby bush and began scratching around in the dirt underneath it. As he did, some tiny white creatures that Cameron thought resembled corn flakes began to wiggle their way up and began to scatter. The creature started slurping them up and seemed to be quite fond of them.

"Eww!" exclaimed Cameron. "I don't know what those things are but I think I'm going to have to be a little hungrier before I try *them*." He thought for a moment as his new friend began digging up more of the little 'white flake creatures'. After seeing the animal enjoy even more of them he reconsidered and reached out and stamped on one of them. He slowly put it to his mouth. "What the heck." he said. "I've already eaten bugs, how bad could this be?" He gingerly began to chew the thing and thought it wasn't half bad. It wasn't half good either but he thought a large number of them cooked in a sauce over an open flame might become a tad more palatable.

"Thank you little friend." said Cameron addressing the creature. "You've opened me up to a new food possibility. Of course me being the new kid in town I could probably learn a lot more from you." He thought for a moment and continued. "You ought to have a name or something. What should I call you... what should I call you?" He stood watching the creature continue digging for his breakfast. "Well you like to dig, don't you? I think I'll call you Digger. No, that's too silly. How about Digby? Yeah, that's it. Digby! It's got character to it. Now that you have a name I can stop worrying about what the heck you are, right Digby?" He then reached down to pat Digby on the head to which the creature turned back and snapped at him. "Whoa! Sorry there buddy. I should know better than to bother a wild animal when it's eating. I don't like to be bothered while I'm eating either."

Cameron gathered quite a few of the 'white flakes' as he called them and put them away in the tree house. He figured they would be safe there out of Digby's reach. Digby's short legs could barely get him over a small stump so the tree house was definitely out of range. After doing that he jumped back down to the ground and decided to look for something to go along with the new dish. He remembered a place where he'd seen several bushes that had quite a few berries on them. Since he had no storage he had left most of the berries there on the bush so he assumed there would be plenty still remaining. He thought they might do well as a sauce with the 'white flakes'. But first he decided to get some more water so he headed off to the river. "Hey Digby, want some water boy?" Cam asked, not knowing Digby's gender. "C'mon with me boy. We're going to the river to get some water." Having finished his feast Digby turned around and began walking behind Cameron.

"Atta boy Digby. You're leg's doing much better. You'll be back to your old self in no time. Then again I don't really know what that was since I found you like this. Oh well. Looks like you won't have any trouble followin' me to the river."

Cameron went off toward the river with Digby close behind. Cam walked a little slower than normal so that Digby would not get too far out of sight. He would forget every once in a while and look back to see Digby trying to catch up. Soon they were close enough to the river to hear its waters rushing by. "Not long now Digby 'ol boy!" Cam said as he looked behind to see Digby losing a little steam. "We're almost there and then we can rest a good while."

As he cleared some broken branches in front of him, Cameron thought he heard a noise. It was difficult to make out over the sound of the river but he stopped and looked around to make sure. When he continued to make his way forward through the branches a giant spear came hurtling at his feet. "Holy crap!" Cam yelled as he fell backwards. He got up to find two large figures running toward him. The first one had an overly large bird shaped head and was rapidly being overtaken by his companion. The second one resembled a bear but with more of a reptilian face and claws. He was the one who threw the spear and was quickly heading for Cameron. Cameron gathered himself enough to reach out and grab the spear out of the ground in front of him before the others could get to it.

The spear was twice as large as the one Cameron had made. It was a serious weapon that could easily impale a deer unlike Cameron's which was used for small fish. Even though it was heavier it was light enough that Cam could still swing it about. It gave him a sense of power and courage once he felt it in his grasp. He aimed the pointy end at his oncoming attacker and began to run. The bear-like creature dove at the last second sending Cameron tripping over him and diving right towards the other creature that let out a terrifying shriek as the spear went deep within him. Before Cameron could yank it out the other creature had come around behind him and grabbed his arms. Cam leapt up and kicked backwards towards his attackers' midsection. The beast growled with fury and loosened his grip enough to let Cam go. Cam then managed to get the spear out of the rapidly dying creature and started swinging it at the other one. The monster backed up with its arms in the air. Still feeling the adrenaline flowing Cam lashed out at the creature, striking it across the arm opening a large gash. He then stepped in closer to take another jab only to feel his legs give out beneath him.

Two more creatures had joined in on the attack. One of them, looking like a part human part goat with massive amounts of scar tissue had just rammed Cameron in the back of the legs causing him to fall. The other one had a face where his stomach should be and growing out from where his shoulders should have been were two rather large and craggy horns. He moved in on Cam with a spiked club. Cam lifted the spear up to block the club coming down on him. He rolled over to get to his feet only to find four more odd shaped creatures armed with more spears and clubs coming toward him. At this point he realized he didn't have a chance. He looked up to see if he could escape into the trees. He tried to make a break for it by jumping off the chest of the bear like creature to where he could grab a branch and lift himself up. But before he could get all the way up into the tree he felt something grab at his leg. He looked back to see several creatures leaping up at him and before he knew it he was back on the ground struggling to get free as they bound his arms and legs and threw him in a sack. During the scuffle Samuel's portal key fell out of Cam's pocket although he was too preoccupied to notice it.

The creatures carried him to a tunnel that went under the river. There they made their way south toward the Unfinished Lands. Inside the sack Cameron stopped his struggling. "Well..." he thought to himself, "...this is pretty much it. There's nothing I can do about it. Now I know how Taylor felt in 'Planet of the Apes'. Maybe I'll get a moment where I can escape later. But for now all I can do is go along for the ride." He kept quiet for most of the trip since realizing the creatures either didn't understand him or just didn't respond. "Man, these things stink."

They marched for what seemed like several hours before reaching a large cavern sunk into the ground behind a large clumping of gnarled trees. The opening of the cavern was quite huge to say the least with room enough to walk a half dozen elephants through it side by side. Inside there were large intricate wall paintings. They also had all kinds of carvings made out of the trees that lined the painted walls. There was carved furniture made to fit the odd shapes and sizes of the strange beings. Cameron was unable to see much however through the sack. He could tell they were moving around a corner and then they took him down a large corridor at the end of which was what seemed like a jail cell. They opened up the door and dumped him in, sack and all.

"Hello?" screamed Cameron. "I'm still bound up in here! A little help! Whatever! Don't I even get a phone call? What's with you people? Oh right. These aren't people." Cam managed to wiggle out of the sack and was able to crawl up on a crude bench. Outside the bars he could see two large creatures sitting at a table, presumably guards. They had been successful in their attempts to ignore him. He struggled with his bonds which were nothing more than ropes made of dried vines. "This place is disgusting! What kind of freakin' world is this? They've got giant talkin' monkeys and monsters that can't say anything. I wish I knew what they were gonna do with me. Then again, maybe I don't."

Cam stopped squirming and slumped over. He thought about Digby and hoped that he had gotten away without getting hurt. Then, for the first time since his first day in Gwerinatha, he sulked.

Chapter 8
The Rescue

Cam could not help but stare at the two guards who sat outside his cell. During the scuffle that got him captured he hadn't really had time to look his attackers over. Now with nothing to do but stare he noticed just how different the citizens of the Unfinished Lands really were. One of the guards had goat like features and terribly rough skin. This was the one who knocked Cam down from behind. He was dressed in tattered green rags with a gold belt that had carvings of what appeared to be animal bones. Cam thought it had to have been made by a talented craftsman. He looked up at Cam several times as if to show his distaste for being the target of Cam's staring. Cam didn't blink. He was agitated, frustrated and frankly couldn't believe what he was seeing. The other guard reminded Cam of pictures of giant sloths he had seen in library books. Cam didn't know what to call it; he had spent more time looking at pictures than doing any actual reading. The thing was dressed in a purple tunic which looked much neater than the garb of the other creature. It had no tears and was clean by comparison. Its hair or fur as it were was neatly groomed and it paid far less attention to Cameron than did the goat creature.

Not knowing his fate and surmising that it couldn't be good, Cam tried to be brave about the whole thing. He wasn't going to surrender quietly if he got to the point where he thought his life might be in danger. He had survived too well during the last few weeks in this strange new land to give up that easily. His staring grew more and more intent. He even began to sneer at his captors but no matter what Cam did they kept ignoring him making Cam all the more curious as to what they wanted with him in the first place.

A noise just around the corner got the attention of the guards. They both jumped up from their seats and stood at the ready. Cam didn't take his eyes off of them. Whatever the disturbance was he wasn't going to worry about it in his current predicament.

Then the noise got louder. It sounded like fighting. It was coming closer. The guards started spinning around as if they didn't know what to do. Should they stay and guard the prisoner or see what was happening just around the corner? They didn't have time to make a decision before the fighting came to them. Two figures that seemed to be shaped like apes but with completely smooth skin came bursting around the corner and attacked the guards. The figures were solid gray in hue and Cameron wasn't sure if they even had any faces. Their appearance definitely got his attention however. He had stopped staring down the guards and watched in amazement as the two gray combatants took out the guards with little trouble. After they dispatched the guards they moved over to Cam's cell. They took the keys from the guards and opened the door for him. Cam stood up and went to the back of his cell fearing the worst. But after they opened the door he could sense they were no longer in attack mode. They seemed calm and reserved. Cameron slowly walked out of the cell between the two gray figures. They didn't touch him.

Cam looked at first one and then the other. He could tell now that they were close that they really didn't have any faces, only smooth contours where the eyes, ears and nose would be. They let him move past and were motionless. Before he could fully grasp just what he was looking at he heard a voice break the tense silence.

"Well now, are you ready to be free again?" the voice said.

Cam looked up and saw a human figure walking around the corner. He had a long white cloak trimmed in yellow. He stood several inches taller than Cameron and was narrow of waist and broad of shoulder. His hair was blond and he had bright blue eyes. Cam's first thoughts were of stories he had heard about people getting taken up into UFOs and having humans that assisted the aliens that looked much like this. He was then reminded of his studies of Scandinavia several years earlier in elementary school. He was shocked and excited to see another human face. His mind traveled everywhere in an instant and he had no idea what to say. Finally he came hurtling back to the present when the man repeated his question.

"Well, are you?"

The man reached out to Cam and pulled out a knife with which to cut Cam's bonds. "Give me your hands." he said. Cam lifted them up so that he could cut away his vine ropes that were now scratching his skin terribly. He then let the man continue by cutting through the vines around his ankles as well.

"Now then, you are free." said the man as he gestured with his hand for Cameron to walk forward. Cam stepped away from the cell and began rubbing his wrists. He couldn't help but stare at the faceless allies of his benefactor. "Do not be put off by my assistants. They are not real in the sense that you and I are. They will not harm you."

"Okay..." Cam said as he slowly took a step backwards. "Shouldn't we be getting out of here?"

"Yes." answered the stranger. "Some of these nasties will be quite enraged when they awake. But some of them will not be waking up again. I will take you to my home. You shall be my guest."

Cameron still looked a little scared even though he was trying his best not to show it. "How rude of me not to introduce myself." the man said as he held out his hand. "I am called Jules."

"Cameron." Cam answered as he shook Jules' hand vigorously. Cameron stared at the man intently. He was a bit put off by the aristocratic accent and wondered how he could look so kempt after leading an attack in such a dirty place.

"Now then, let's be off." Jules said as he motioned for his gray assistants to move in front of them. They walked out of the cavern and Cameron finally got a good look at the surroundings. "Quite impressive isn't it?" asked Jules. "It is especially so when you consider how odd some of these creatures look. They are not all bad you know. They're quite intelligent really."

"Well they aren't so good at first impressions." Cam replied.

"I can obviously understand from your perspective." Jules said. "But believe me they were as scared of you as you were of them. Otherwise they wouldn't have locked you away."

"Well I wouldn't say I was *scared* of them." insisted Cameron. "But what you say makes sense I guess. I mean obviously if they had to lock me up they were definitely afraid of me. But what would they have done if you hadn't saved me?"

"Not sure really." replied Jules. He quickly cocked his head at an angle as he looked back at Cameron eyes half open. "But you would not have been treated as nicely as I will treat you once we arrive at my palace."

"*Palace?*" asked Cam. "I haven't seen anything like a palace around here."

"Yes, well you haven't seen much of this place yet then have you?" asked Jules.

"No. I really haven't been here too long." said Cam. "I'm not from this world."

"As I suspected from your clothes and dialect." replied Jules. "We can have a long chat about where you're from on the way to my palace. It's not too far really and I'm quite intrigued by your mysterious origins."

Cam followed Jules and his two assistants out of the cavern and along through the Unfinished Lands back to the palace of the Originators. Along the way Cameron filled Jules in on Robert and the dimensional doorway key and how he had arrived there. Jules was most interested in hearing about America and the more advanced technology with which he was familiar. But it was difficult for Cam to concentrate as they made their way back.

He thought he noticed in some areas grass that was moving independently of the ground beneath it. He saw large rocks jutting through the dirt that seemed to grow and shrink. Trees were moving around in circles and the closer they got to the palace the stranger things got. All the while through sightings of the strange features of the Unfinished Lands Jules seemed undistracted. He told him not to worry. He explained to him that he was safe as long as he followed closely and stuck with him. He assured him that he had lived here long enough to be aware of the dangers that surrounded him and that he knew where and when it was safe to walk.

This seemed to placate Cameron and he began to feel more confident as they continued. What he didn't notice during the walk however was the metamorphosis taking place in Jules' assistants. The natural occurrences in topography of the Unfinished Lands was distracting enough but Jules' insistence on hearing about his homeland made it so that his attention was strained. It wasn't until they reached the palace that he noticed the assistants were getting a little slower that he gave them a second glance. Their skin was no longer smooth but was now rough and craggy. They were no longer gray but a mottled mess of gray, black and rust. It seemed also that they were getting just a little bit smaller. They had been changing ever so slowly during the trip back. Once they got to the door of the palace Jules simply motioned his hands at them and they crumbled to dust.

"What the...?" exclaimed Cameron.

"Not to worry." replied Jules. "As I said before, they were not real in the sense that you and I are. They were just *temporary* workers. "

"Okay..." said Cameron as they walked into the palace.

Cameron was given a tour of the palace. Jules didn't spend much time on the grand hall or the throne room; instead he took him briefly to each of the various floors showing him the vastness of the building. Then he spent more time showing him the living quarters. Finally he brought him to a large room with an ornate bed and large windows. "This, Cameron, is your room." Jules told him. "If you would like it that is."

Cameron looked around and tried not show Jules how excited he was. "It's fantastic!"

"I hope you do not mind that I am being a bit presumptuous." said Jules. "But you see there really isn't any safe place for you to live out there. I am the last of my kind and am very lonely so I do hope you'll take me up on my offer."

"Well, I don't know... I mean, I..." Cam stuttered.

"I understand." Jules responded. "I do not require an immediate answer nor do I expect one. Suffice it to say that you are free to live here for as long as you wish. Once you get to know the Unfinished Lands a little better you'll see that this is definitely where you will wish to stay."

***

In the forest where the struggle had taken place with Cameron the portal key had been found by the giant monkey. At first the bemused primate held it up to the sun. "What sort of a strange thing is this I wonder?" he wondered. The jewels on the key began to gradually get brighter. "There's something you don't see everyday." A rift in space slowly began to open in front of the monkey. At first it was no bigger than a pebble and within seconds as large as a fist. "Egads! What sort of bizarre occurrence is this?" he muttered.

The monkey peered through the growing rift while still holding the key up. "I say, there seems to be another world entirely through this little strange occurrence floating cleverly in front of me." He saw an eye peering back at him. He then shrieked, fell over backwards and as the key flew out of his paw the rift promptly vanished. "Well now since that is the sort of thing you don't see everyday I should think I'll not see it again for some time." He spent a minute or so pacing in circles around the key. "What to do, what to do, with this strange little thing? What could this be used for I wonder?" he wondered aloud yet again. He then picked up the key and started swinging it around and around. He tossed it up in the air a few times and then began to look at it more closely. He turned it on its side and looked at it with one eye closed. He then held it up to the tip of his nose and balanced it there. He liked to see it wiggle but then noticed the jewels glowing again and quickly stopped. As he brought it down out of the light he noticed the jewels grew dim again. He took it and rubbed the short end around and around the inside of each of his ears. It was precisely at the moment he thought of a use for the thing. He decided it would be a handy tool to dislodge hewlifruits from the upper branches of the hewlifruit trees. "I imagine this to be a wonderful thing. Yes. Yes indeed that is what the new use of my strange little thing shall be. I shall call it, 'tool'." And with that the monkey set off in search of hewlifruits.

Chapter 9
The Great Hunter

Cameron spent little time making his decision. A few short trips out into the Unfinished Lands accompanied with the memories of his struggles in Anhysbys Forest made it an easy choice. Jules spent many years training Cameron how to survive in the Unfinished Lands. He taught him how to fight against the many different creatures that inhabit them. This was made all the easier with the assistance of the temporary figures supplied by Jules. Cameron not only lost the uneasiness he felt around them but came to rely on them in combat. He still felt somewhat odd when they would crumble to dust but he came to understand when that was going to happen and was able to use it to his advantage. To better cope with the experience Cameron would give them numbers as names. Even without them he still had confidence in his abilities combating the strange denizens of the Unfinished Lands. Jules helped him discern which were friendly and which were not whenever Cameron had difficulty in that area. The friendliest of course being those who were descended from the original life forms created by the Originators and not those from the accursed ones though this historical detail was not explained to him by Jules. No matter how harsh the battles may have been, Cam knew there was always a comfortable room awaiting him back in the palace.

Cameron lived like a prince. In fact, that is how Jules came to think of him. He had explained that all that was his was now Cameron's and he should consider himself ruler of all the land. Cam felt like he had everything he could want. He was given smart Gwerinathan clothing and had all he could ask for in terms of food. Jules had also provided Cameron with a stable of horses exactly like the ones he remembered from home, far different from the Gwerinathan horses with their beaks and talons which Cameron had yet to encounter. He even managed to find Digby lurking about on one of his hunting trips. Digby became a constant companion to Cameron and had his own outdoor home nearby the castle in the stable part of the Unfinished Lands. Digby was now full grown and was the size of a large dog. Cameron still didn't have a clue as to what type of creature he was and thought he hadn't grown more attractive with age but still had affection for him just the same. Digby's legs were large enough now that he could almost keep up with a horse so Cameron would occasionally take him on some of his hunting trips. He wasn't really too much help with his long neck and tail and was much better in finding flake creatures and truffles than prey suited for a human appetite. Still, Cameron liked the company.

On the eve of his twelfth year in the palace, Jules had decided to have a feast in order to celebrate. Cameron, who thought of Jules now as a surrogate father, was grateful but insisted on supplying the main course, fresh venison. So he took off toward Anhysbys Forest along with two temporary assistants, Six Forty Seven and Six Forty Eight he called them, to help carry back the deer. Digby followed close behind. Digby didn't much care for the terrain of the Unfinished Lands but knew if he stuck close to Cameron he would always be safe.

After making it to the edge of the forest Cameron had Six Forty Eight stay behind with the horse while the rest of them went ahead. Cameron had made a camouflaged cloak that he would use to cover himself with while waiting for deer. He had several spots hidden away in certain trees with good vantage points that he would hide in. At one such tree he climbed up with the cloak after sending Digby up with Six Forty Seven. Once he climbed up, he covered the three of them with the cloak and waited patiently.

Cameron's hunting weapon of choice was the bow. He had gone with his uncle on a couple of bow hunting trips back home and found the experience in Gwerinatha was not too dissimilar. Of course he had never worried about talking animals or moving trees at home but the deer themselves acted very much the same. In fact, deer were one of very few animals that Cam could recognize as being the same. The horses certainly weren't and he still hadn't a clue as to what his friend Digby was let alone most of the inhabitants of the Unfinished Lands. Because of the deer's familiarity, hunting them was a comforting pastime for Cameron.

He waited patiently about an hour or so before spotting a deer. This particular deer was quite large and excited Cam a great deal. He worried that it was not going to come close enough to get a good shot at it. Then he worried that it was coming at the wrong angle and that he wasn't going to be able to maneuver himself into proper position to shoot it. He noticed the deer seemed agitated. It began twitching and sniffing the air. "What's wrong with that thing." Cam thought to himself. "It's not acting right. It's like it's nervous or something." Cam wasn't sure what to make of the deer's actions. He knew he and his party had remained quiet so the deer couldn't have been spooked by them. He figured he'd only get the one shot so even though his angle was a bit uncomfortable he pulled back on his bow string, arrow at the ready.

He let go the arrow and it whizzed right past the deer's midsection causing it to jump away in fright. At that moment two wolves began howling in the distance. The two near simultaneous events startled Cam to the point he fell out of the tree. Six Forty Seven grabbed his leg as he fell keeping him from hitting the ground. Cam was then able to grab hold of the trunk of the tree and climb to the ground on his own.

"What the heck was that?" said Cam no longer worried about keeping silent. "That sounded like wolves howling!" He then quieted his tone. "I haven't seen any wolves yet in this strange place. But I'm pretty sure that's what that sound was."

"That's exactly right sir." a voice called out from the distance. "Nor should you be *seeing* wolves in this place because you humans shouldn't be hunting in Anhysbys Forest!"

"Who said that?" asked Cameron.

The two wolves came out from behind some trees several yards away. One of them, tall and proud, stepped in front of the other. "I did." he proclaimed.

"Who... what are you?" Cam stuttered.

"The better question is who *you* are and *what* you are doing in Anhysbys Forest when no human dares to hunt here." the wolf answered. "It's bad enough you have started to hunt more in Serenity Forest and have moved us to the strange and inconsistent hunting grounds here. Now you have scared off my family's dinner as well."

"I beg to differ wolf but that buck was going to be *my* dinner." Cam retorted.

"Why can't you leave us alone? There are plenty of deer in the other forests." the second wolf shouted in a feminine voice.

"Been a while since I've run into any talking animals." Cam said. "I don't mean to argue with you guys but I really would like that buck for a special dinner in my honor."

"I don't argue with humans." The first wolf exclaimed. "...and that buck was to be dinner for my family as I said before. Nothing special mind you but deer *is* our particular favorite. So if you'd be so kind as to move on I won't report you as a poacher."

"Poacher?" Cam questioned rhetorically. "You have got to be kidding me! A wolf calling *me* a poacher?"

"You have no rights in Anhysbys Forest." the second wolf called out.

"You should be more than aware of that sir." the first wolf added.

"I don't know what you're talking about." Cam replied. "I've never had trouble like this before but I can tell you I'm ready to handle it!" With that, Cam whistled a signal for his assistant to come down out of the tree and help him fight off the wolves. Cam drew a knife meant to gut the deer and ran at them. Six Forty Seven jumped from out of the tree and ran close behind.

The wolves did not back down. They both ran after their attackers, teeth showing and prepared to clamp down hard if necessary. Cam swung hard at the first wolf that jumped right over his slashing arm. The second wolf grabbed at Six Forty Seven's arm and bit down hard. He swung around flipping the wolf over. The wolf let out a yelp and let go of the gray arm. Machine like, Six Forty Seven picked the wolf up and with his ape like arms hurtled it toward a tree. The wolf hit the tree and yelped again. At that, the first wolf, now angrier took off after Six Forty Seven and lunged for his chest. He knocked the thing down and bit at its arm until it started to come apart. The arm now was hanging like it was attached with a rubber band that had lost its elasticity. He reached out with his other arm to grab the wolf around its middle but the wolf kicked back with his hind legs, jumping off Six Forty Seven toward Cameron who was now headed toward the injured second wolf by the tree.

"Oh no you don't!" yelled the wolf as he jumped up and bit Cameron's hand causing him to drop the knife.

"Aggh!!" yelled Cameron as he fell over in pain. Cam rolled over and reached for the knife with his left hand. While he did that Six Forty Seven with his dangling arm, which was now changing to various shades of gray, started toward the first wolf again. The wolf lunged forward and bit the creature's neck. At once Six Forty Seven turned solid black and crumbled to dust on the ground.

"What in Gwerinatha?" shouted the first wolf, staring in

disbelief at what had happened.

Just then he heard a yelp and turned to see Cameron slashing at his partner. "Stop!" yelled the first wolf as he ran behind him and began to growl. "I do not wish to harm any human. It is against my nature but I will not hesitate to take your life to save that of my mate!"

Cameron stopped attacking the second wolf which was limping and bleeding from a cut on her legs. He turned to face the first wolf. "I don't back down easy." Cam said almost mumbling now.

"And I don't back down at all... not when it comes to saving a member of my pack."

"So what do we do now?" asked Cameron.

"You leave." stated the wolf simply. "It's up to you whether your pride goes with you. But you've done enough damage here today and I do not wish to see you again!"

Cameron stared menacingly at the wolf for a minute or two. He realized the wolf was serious about not backing down and he also was still smarting from the bite on his hand. He also knew his other gray assistant was too far away to hear him and come to his aid. He also didn't want to risk getting Digby hurt so he began to slowly back away. "Fine." he said smugly. "But you haven't seen the last of me. I'll be back and I'll hunt in this forest whenever I like! I promise you!"

The wolves stared at him as he walked back to the tree. They said nothing as he slowly climbed up and got Digby leaving his bow and arrows in the tree and continued on out of the forest. "I'm just glad you're safe Digby." Cam said as he stroked Digby's head. "If they'd harmed you I would have torn them limb from limb!" Digby cooed a little and after they had gotten out of sight of the wolves Cameron set him on the ground to walk alongside of him.

Chapter 10
Louie's Concern

In a wolf den in Anhysbys Forest a small pack of wolves waited impatiently. Their pack leader, Louie was late in coming back from the hunt with his mate Maria. "The pups are getting anxious Sophie." said an older female wolf pacing impatiently back and forth across the den.

"I am too." Sophie replied. "They aren't usually gone this long."

Just then Louie and Maria howled in the distance and the wolves dropped their worry. This new pack, recently formed, had had its struggles. Hunting in Anhysbys Forest could be worrisome but the hunting in Serenity Forest had become scarce considering the humans had begun to hunt there and there were still a few older packs left there as well. One of those older packs was headed by Wendy, Louie's older sister. She still had a den not too far away from their one near Branwen's Garden. Wendy had taken over the pack after their grandfather, Arthur, had passed on. Their brother Richard had long since started another pack in the far western part of Serenity Forest. With the humans now encroaching on Serenity Forest Louie had no choice but to look elsewhere to form his own pack.

Anhysbys Forest could be dangerous however as it was so large and so close to the Unfinished Lands. There were still large sections of the forest that had gone unexplored and many strange creatures were known to lurk about including a rarely seen giant monkey that was thought to live only in the canopy. The only positive thing about it was that no humans were brave enough to have ever thought of hunting there. At least that is what the wolves had always thought.

Louie had dragged most of the hindquarters of a large buck behind him. Maria began regurgitating some of what she had already eaten for the pups who were already jumping up and down in front of her. Before Louie could begin to tell the wolves where the rest of the carcass was hidden he was getting a scolding. "What took you so long father?" asked Sophie. "We were beginning to worry. The pups are starving!"

"Calm down daughter!" said Louie. "I have been scolded enough in my life by my elders. I won't have my own pup speaking to me that way."

"Sorry, father." replied Sophie. "But I am not a pup you know. I have been full grown for over a season now!"

"And so much like me when I was your age too." said Louie. "I wish I could tell you we were late for no good reason but we discovered men hunting here in Anhysbys Forest!"

"What?!" screamed Sophie. "Not here!"

"Not men exactly..." Maria said as she walked past the pups now filling their stomachs with their partially predigested meal. She gave Louie a slight scowl as she walked over to her eldest daughter. "...man. There was only *one* man to be specific. You know how your father is."

"Yes, but he wasn't alone." added Louie.

"True, there was a strange creature with him." said Maria. "...like nothing I've seen before."

"Mother, you're hurt!" exclaimed Sophie noticing her mother's limp and bleeding legs.

"I'm all right." she responded. "...just a scratch!"

"No. It's worse than that." replied Sophie.

"I think Sophie's right dear." said Louie. "You put up a brave front for the younger ones but I think we should have your legs tended to. We'll head right away to Serenity Forest where we can get help."

Louie made sure the older wolves in his pack were safe and explained that he didn't believe the human would have followed him. He convinced them that there wouldn't be any trouble and had them promise to take care of the young pups. He then took his mate to their original home in Serenity Forest. On the way she noticed a strange look in his eyes. "There's something else isn't there Louie?" she asked him.

"What do you mean?"

"My legs aren't that bad." she told him. "I can use some aid from the wildlife defenders but it's not crucial. You're thinking of something else you won't tell me about. I know you too well Louie."

"You're right." he answered. "It was that man. There was something strangely familiar about him. I'm hoping to find Seren in Branwen's garden today. I need to talk to her about it."

As night fell they reached Serenity Forest. They ran into a pack led by Louie's older brother, Richard. It was not uncommon for packs to fight over territory even if they are related. Richard stared down his younger brother but then backed off somewhat after seeing Maria's obvious limp. After convincing Richard they were not trying to hunt in their territory they were allowed to spend the night. When morning came they were off to Branwen's Garden. When they got there Louie saw a few trusted members of the wildlife defenders who had helped them before. They immediately tended to Maria while Louie looked around.

Louie noticed a familiar face gathering vegetables from the garden. It was Charity, the youngest of Seren's sisters who had spent more time than the others in the garden. He approached her and received a big hug as Charity had considered him a long time family friend.

"Oh Louie, it's been ages!" Charity shrieked. "It's fantastic to see you again. I'm all squeaks and giggles!"

"Wonderful to see you as always Charity." Louie replied. "Has Seren been 'round?"

"Something's wrong isn't it?" asked Charity. "I can tell."

"I'm not sure." Louie said quietly. "I need to speak with Seren if she's about."

"She's actually planning on coming in this afternoon as matter of fact." replied Charity. "What is it? Can't I be of assistance? You know how much I like to help out."

It's not that." Louie said. "I think I'll just wait for Seren. In the meantime tell me what's been going on with you."

Louie intentionally changed the subject knowing that Charity would not let it go if he didn't. He then got her to talking about her family and how Mercy and Grace were doing with their husbands and children. He knew he'd get pretty good mileage out of having her chatting about her nieces and nephews. He then found out that she was engaged to be married which took her mind even further from Louie's concern. Charity loved to talk and her sisters were a favorite subject. She went on about how strange it was that Seren was the only one of her family not romantically attached to anyone. Mercy and Grace had told her they believed it was because she took her role as Branwen's replacement in the wildlife defender's group too seriously and that her convictions made her too busy for romance. But Charity believed there was something else, something that Seren would never speak about to the others. Louie smiled thinking he knew what that might be and happy that Charity was no longer asking him questions just as he had hoped.

Eventually Seren showed up and after having family time with her sister Louie finally got a few minutes alone with her to speak. He told her of how he and Maria came to be there and the thought of humans hunting in Anhysbys Forest seemed to bother her as much as it did Louie. The description of the gray ape like faceless being wasn't very comforting to her either.

"This is more than disturbing." said Seren. "I've never heard of anything like what you described. It sounds like nothing we'd seen before even during our unfortunate time in the Unfinished Lands. And why would humans be hunting in Anhysbys Forest? You also heard him say he's been there before, many times?"

"From what I understood." answered Louie. "But that's not the worst of it. He was dressed in clothes that were similar to your people but there was something *different* about him."

"What do you mean, Louie?"

"I couldn't put my paw on it at first. But I thought about it after we got back to our den. It was the way he spoke. I think you'd call it a dialect."

"His dialect?" asked Seren. "What are you talking about?"

"I'd only ever heard one other person speak that way." he answered. "It's been so many years that it took a while to sink in."

"You mean...?"

"Yes." Louie replied. "He spoke just like Robert."

Seren sat back and looked toward the sky. Her thoughts drifted back to the young boy who dropped in seemingly out of nowhere and helped save her sister, Branwen, only to have Branwen sacrifice herself for him. Seren had thought of Robert many times since then. She missed him terribly at times. Her sisters all had said at one time or another that she was pining away for him and was being unfair to the many available suitors who regularly had sought her affections. At nearly twenty seven years of age she was very much an old maid by Gwerinathan standards. It didn't matter much to her though. She knew deep down however that it was true. How could any boy in Gwerinatha match up to a boy from another world? She could still remember the descriptions of America and how wonderful it all sounded to her. She always imagined what it must be like to ride in an automobile, to see a movie on a giant screen or to have shoes with no laces. Her mind was brought crashing back to the present by Louie's questioning.

"What do you think, Seren? Could another from Robert's world have traveled here?

"I don't know Louie. I just don't know. Either way, having humans in Anhysbys Forest ought to be investigated. This definitely needs to be brought to Samuel's attention.

Chapter 11
Who Are These People?

Cameron had just put Digby into his house and stormed for the door of the palace. He was so angry he almost slammed the door on Six Forty Eight who had already shown signs of being near the end of his cycle. He rushed up the stairs past Granton, who was on his way down with a tray of tea. He headed to the living quarters and threw himself on his bed.

Granton, still young looking by the occasional recharges Gule would give him, had become known to Cameron as the 'family butler'. In fact Cam would sometimes joke and call him 'Mr. French' after the only butler he knew from his childhood television viewing. Granton could obviously tell something was troubling Cameron and decided to report it to Gule rather than deal with it himself. Although Granton put up a good front for Cameron he still hated humans and would only speak to him if ordered by Gule or in case of emergencies. Being called 'Mr. French' didn't help the situation any.

Granton entered the 'war room' where Gule was in the middle of another of his long deep thinking trances. "Set the tea down and be gone Granton." Gule said in a slow and tired manner. Granton remained but wouldn't speak and wondered if it might be better to speak than to annoy Gule by disobeying his order. Before he could ponder it long enough to come to a proper conclusion Gule spoke again. "Why are you still here?" he asked without even looking at him. Gule slowly turned his head and with his eyes half closed he stared down at Granton. He seemed more disappointed than angry. "Do you have some news from outside?"

"Not exactly, sire." Granton said quietly. "It is Cameron. He has arrived home from the hunt and seems particularly disturbed."

"Yes, yes. I heard him enter. How could I not?" Gule said with eyes rolling. "Go back to your duties. I shall tend to Cameron in my own good time."

Granton took his leave of the 'war room' and headed back to the living quarters. As he headed back up the stairs he saw Cameron running down them in a huff. He quickly found something to occupy his time as he knew he did not want to be anywhere near Gule and

Cameron during what he expected to be a confrontation.

Hearing the young man running down the stairs Gule became irritated. He threw his cloak up over his head and began to move back and forth as if he were in a sort of chrysalis. The whole room had a bright glow of yellow light filling it. The light grew brighter and brighter and then the room returned to normal. When it did Gule's cloak came down to reveal Jules in his place. Jules cricked his neck and moved his shoulders up and down as if just waking from an abnormally long sleep. He then rubbed his now human looking eyes tightly as Cameron entered the room. "Ah, Cameron. I thought I heard you come home. I was just napping a bit."

"Sorry to bother you sir." Cam replied. "I just can't help being angry at the moment. Something weird's goin' on here."

"Sit down my son." Jules said. Whenever Jules wanted to calm Cameron down he would always call him 'son'. It usually had the desired effect but this time Cam still seemed tense. "What is troubling you?"

"First, I have no *deer* for the feast tomorrow." Cam said in an agitated tone. "And second, the reason I *have* no deer is because I encountered some *wolves* that scared it off! And if that wasn't enough these wolves, who could *talk*, told me that *humans* aren't supposed to hunt in the Forest. They called it Aniz-Buh, Aneesba..."

"Anhysbys Forest" Jules finished.

"Yeah. Anhysbys Forest. How did you know that? And how is it there are people around? Do you know about them too?" Cam's tone became more frustrated. "I thought you told me you were the last of your kind. What is goin' on around here?"

"Clearly the time has come to tell you more of this place Cameron." Jules said. "I have tried so very hard to protect you and concealing some information was necessary I'm afraid. I knew I could only do so for a time. I had only hoped this day would come much later than this. What I have to tell you will not be easy to hear."

"Could you get on with it, please?" Cam asked.

"No need for insolence boy." Jules replied in a tone that made Cam nervous. "Yes. I have kept things from you. But I have not lied. I *am* the last of *my* kind. These *humans* that the wolf mentions are not like you and I. Oh they may resemble humans on the outside but trust me when I say that they are *sub*human at best. They are a disease that lives only to destroy all that is good. You see I came here with my people from another world myself. We came here many years ago from a far distant star. I was just a baby when we arrived but I still remember how frightened my parents were when they first encountered the brutally savage inhabitants of this land *they* call Gwerinatha. They came from a different world also. This is not their native land. Whatever brilliance they may have had to get them here has long since died out. The descendants of those that first came here are left with little intelligence but a great deal of savagery.

These sub humans live far away from here in various towns and villages. They forced my parents and their comrades into an area they called the Unfinished Lands. That is where we are now. You recognize how unstable the ground is on your way to and from the forest. You see the trees and rocks moving as if they are alive and you see the odd storms that can rage one instant and be gone the next. It is called unfinished because of some legend they tell of a long gone race of beings that created the land but left before it could be completed. They believe it is a place of much danger and fear it greatly. They would never try to come through here and so here they drove us, the one place we could be safe."

"Safe?" Cameron remarked.

"Yes, safe from *them*. With all the strange creatures you have seen here and all that is dangerous with the environment it is still better than living out there with them. I told you they are not really human. They would sooner kill you than to speak to you. Trust me when I say they are most dangerous." Jules then turned his head and looked sadly down at the floor. "And it is such a pity that the best lands of this world are theirs but there is nothing that can be done about it. I am just fortunate my parents found this one stable place to build this wonderful palace to remind them of home. It took them and their friends dozens of years to complete it. Sadly they didn't get to enjoy it for very long before..."

"Before what?"

"Before their lives were brutally taken from them by the sub humans." Jules got up and slowly walked towards a window. He leaned against the sill and gestured toward the pane with an open hand. "Each time any of us wandered out past the Unfinished Lands they would be killed. In a matter of years there were only a few of us left and the rest of them have died of old age or recklessness wandering the Unfinished Lands. I am all that remains of my people."

Jules walked away from the window and stood proudly in the center of the room. His melancholy swiftly changed to a sense of great confidence. "I have become stronger by living in these Unfinished Lands. They have made me stronger than the subhumans." Jules walked over to Cameron who was still sitting at the foot of his throne. He reached down and grabbed his chin with his thumb and index finger while staring gently into his eyes. "You are like me Cameron I can tell. The way you speak, your intelligence, it's all so very different from them." Jules then walked back to the center of the room leaving Cameron with a strange look on his face. "We can live safely here in the palace. We can hunt in Anhysbys Forest for food because that is one of the last places in all of Gwerinatha outside the Unfinished Lands that they will ever go. You do not have to worry about them."

Cam thought about it for a moment. He thought he would ask another question about the humans but put it out of his mind. "What about the wolves then?" he asked.

"Yes, well I suppose with a few of my temporaries at your side you could manage to take out a few wolves here and there. I can make plenty of them you see. My father's technology actually. He was a very brilliant man. Yes, I usually only make two at a time because that's all we really need. In fact I had about seven I believe when I first rescued you but only two were left by the time we got to you. I could actually make twenty, thirty or even fifty at a time if we needed them, a whole army."

"A whole army?" Cam wondered.

"Yes." Jules said. "*If* they were needed.

Jules let his words sink in for a moment. He knew that Cameron had a great deal to think about. "Have some tea Cameron." Jules said handing him a cup on the tray left by Granton. "It will calm you. Then go back to your room and rest for a while. I am sure that you are tired after your ordeal and all I have told you cannot help your jangled nerves. So please calm down and do not dwell on what I have told you. Tomorrow we will celebrate your twelfth anniversary here with us and all will be well."

"Fine." said Cameron as he took a sip of tea. "I'll try not to worry about it but that's an awful lot to think about."

"Yes." Jules said. "I know…"

Chapter 12
Heavy is the Head

"Another stack of papers?" questioned Samuel after an aide dropped them on an already cluttered desk. "It never ends. I thought things were bad enough when I took on the advisor role to Governor Baylies but this new governor who has taken over after his death needs even more attention." Samuel stopped a moment to remember his friend, Padrig Baylies. It had been several years since his death from a heart attack. Samuel had told him many times to watch his overeating and sedentary lifestyle but his words seemed to him to fall on deaf ears. He wondered if there could have been more that he could have done but he had seen so many people pass in his extremely long life and it never got easier. That was one thing he missed about his self imposed exile. No funerals, no eulogies, no mourning.

"I'm sorry sir," the aide said. "but it has to do with the dam to be built for the Village of Idiots."

"Yes, yes I know. But it's all gotten far too complicated. When I first came here and we needed a dam built we'd build the blasted thing. There was no need to go forming committees and creating permits and the need for all this paperwork. It's ludicrous."

Samuel pored over the pages left for him. He had solved many of Gwerinatha's problems in the years since his return but building a dam for the Village of Idiots had still remained a sticking point. This new proposal he was now looking at was the first one in many years he thought might actually work. It had been whittled down from a hundred and seventy-two pages to a mere twenty-three in a matter of seven years. Gone were all the cost saving factors the House of Fates argued were going to adversely affect the environment. Gone too were the mandates that the workers had to all be Village of Idiot residents which would adversely affect the craftsmanship of the dam according to the Lords of Wisdom. Both sides felt it an unimportant issue since they didn't consider the residents there first class citizens but now it looked like after many years something may finally be done. "I think we may have something here. Just a few more jots to adjust and..."

Before Samuel could finish his thought Seren had burst into the room, Samuel's aide close behind her. "Samuel!" exclaimed Seren, "I have to speak with you right away. It's urgent!"

"I tried to stop her sir," the aide butted in, "but she was quite insistent."

"That's fine Steffan, she can stay."

"Yes sir." The aide replied, quickly shutting the door behind him.

"Now what's all this about Seren?" asked Samuel. "You can see I am right in the middle of some very important work…"

"Yes. I know that and I am truly sorry but I wouldn't interrupt if I didn't feel it were necessary."

"I know how important the legislation on keeping Anhysbys Forest free from hunting is to you. I have been in dozens of committees hearing both sides of what frankly dear, is growing to be a very tired debate. I can honestly tell you that I haven't…"

"No, no. It's not about that." Seren interrupted. "Well not directly anyway. It's all so very disturbing."

"Here, now. Sit down." Samuel said gesturing Seren to have a seat. "I'll have Steffan bring us a cup of tea. You look moderately upset child. What is this all about then?"

"It's Louie and Maria." she answered. "They were attacked by hunters in Anhysbys Forest."

"Well that can't be." Samuel retorted. "It is illegal for humans to hunt there. At least for now it remains so. Now I know there are those who are up in arms over this issue and are desperately trying to get that law overturned but you don't think any of them would be responsible…"

"No! I don't think it was one of us."

"Whatever do you mean by 'one of us'?

"I mean I don't think anyone from Gwerinatha was involved. I think it was an outsider and more importantly, from Robert's world."

A look of astonishment took out what little color remained in Samuel's face. He thought how impossible that sounded and wanted to ignore it completely. Seren went on to explain in detail what Louie and Maria had told her of their experience giving extra attention to the strange being accompanying the human and his foreign accent. He thought about it for a while and then decided that it shouldn't be a real concern considering the source. "Now you know that I have taken a strong liking to you Seren. You are to me like the daughter I never had and I have especially felt that way in the years since your father's passing. You know I would not council you in haste but since this account does come from a rather incredulous source I don't think it is much to worry about."

"Not much to worry about?" echoed Seren. "But this could be a very dangerous situation! This man could very well be from Robert's world. And if another could have come through it's only logical that many more could follow! Who knows how many of them could be here? They could have weapons we have no defense against. They could end up razing the forest! Who knows what kind of trouble we could be in for?"

"Now, please just calm yourself Seren. I really have a tremendous amount of work to get to as you can see." Samuel said waving his arm over the mess of papers on his desk. He stared lovingly at Seren and then paused. He thought carefully before choosing his next words. He knew Seren was upset and did not want to make the situation worse but felt that he had to let his opinion be known. "I think you may be letting your feelings about Robert blind you to more of Louie's tall tales. I'm sure he and Maria jumped to conclusions and probably did encounter a rogue hunter from one of our villages. I promise you I'll investigate this further..."

"Why does everyone keep thinking I have some sort of feelings for Robert?" Seren yelled. "And what does that have to do with anything anyway? He could have been in some serious trouble to let others back here. You know he would never endanger us!"

"Precisely, my dear. Which is why you shouldn't worry. Now why don't you take a few days and go back to Baylies Crossing and visit your family? I think it would do you good."

"You don't really think this is that serious?"

"At this point, no." said Samuel. "Your cousin Urien is more than capable of taking on any challenge as you well know." Urien had since merged the Southern Guard and his own police service in to what amounted as a military force which had many successful encounters in protecting villagers from savage attacks. "If it makes you feel any better I can tell you that I have all three of the orbs hidden safely away and can get to them if a horrible crisis does indeed arise that should merit their use. I will look into this when I get time. If someone has been hunting illegally in Anhysbys Forest I will personally make sure they are punished under the full extent of the law as it now stands. In fact, I shall make sure that even if the law is overturned they will be punished retroactively. There! Now how does that all sound?"

"I don't know Samuel." Seren replied. "I want to believe you that it's all just me getting carried away but I still feel like there's more to it than just poachers."

"I really have to get back to work Seren." Samuel said as he got up and went to the door. "I promise we'll talk about this again as soon as possible. I'll get in touch with Urien today and make him aware of all that you have told me. I'll see that he investigates this properly. Now go on. I'll see you later."

Samuel then hugged Seren and she quietly walked out the door. He then went back to his desk to work more on the dam proposal. After looking over the papers once again he paused for a moment and looked toward the ceiling. He pondered for a minute, shook his head and then went back to work.

***

High in the highest trees in Anhysbys forest where the hewlifruits grow the giant monkey was busy getting some fruits down for his morning meal. "Oh, I do love my new hewlifruit dislodging tool." he said brightly. "I don't know what I ever did without it."

Then reaching out to an especially large, nearly overripe hewlifruit that was just barely out of arms reach he took the key and poked at the fruit. He just missed it so he moved a little further out on the branch and in so doing dropped the key. He sat silently watching the key fall through the branches of the hewlifruit trees. He listened intently as it made a noise with each leaf and branch it brushed past on its way to the forest floor. After he could see and hear it no more he slowly turned and looked at the luscious hewlifruit still dangling in front of him due to his weight on the branch. He then stretched out a little further and pulled the fruit off the branch. "Now I remember." he said. As he began to eat the hewlifruit he sat back and smiled. "Mmm... This is a particularly good one."

Chapter 13
These People Can't Be For Real

Days had past since Cameron's celebratory feast with Jules. Cameron tried his best to keep a festive spirit but the news of other humans kept eating away at him. He hadn't said anything more to Jules in order to keep the peace. He knew how much the celebration had meant to Jules and he was ever so thankful for all that Jules had done for him. He decided he might try and seek out the humans, informing Jules that he would just be going out hunting again. He assumed his true intentions would not be detected by Jules since he'd not brought the subject up in the interim. He approached Jules just before his usual nap time hoping his being tired would aid the situation.

"Sir," Cameron said quietly. "I have decided to go out hunting again. I have been stuck in here for a few days and could use some fresh air."

"And you'd like to see the humans, wouldn't you?" Jules inquired in a condescending tone.

"Wh-What are you talking about sir?" Cam stuttered. "I'm just going hunting. I won't stray from my usual route. I don't think I want to see those…"

"…those, what?" asked Jules. "Subhumans? Is that what you

were going to say? You do believe me, don't you? You do trust me, don't you son?"

"Well of course, sir. I mean I, uh..."

"Look, I know you want to see the humans with your own eyes. It's only natural. You feel all alone here with just me and a few of the domesticated creatures we allow in the palace. I know. And I do not mind. However, before you go rushing off getting yourself into trouble why don't you allow me to have a few of my temporaries accompany you to the closest village? Let me select the route for you so you will have less chance of wandering into an unsafe area."

Cam shook his head. "I don't know what to say. You don't mind if I go see these people after all you've told me? I would have thought that you'd be angry."

"Angry?" bemused Jules. "I suppose that's natural as well. From my perspective I do have a particularly nasty temperament towards the Gwerinathans. But you *should* see them for yourself. You see I believe that once you see them for yourself, you'll see them as I do. Your curiosity is to be expected and I cannot doubt that deep in your heart you may hold out some hope that they are like you. But you'll see that this cannot be true."

Cam looked down at the floor. He felt as if Jules was somehow reading his mind. But then he figured that it was a very normal parental reaction that Jules was having. At that moment he felt closer to Jules than he ever had to his own father. "I'll go along with whatever plan you have sir." Cam told him. "...and thanks."

"Thanks for what?" asked Jules.

"Just 'thanks'. Cameron said and then walked out of the room in a rush.

Jules exited slowly behind him and headed toward the room where the temporary assistants were created. Cameron got there ahead of him and was waiting patiently. The room was filled with odd looking equipment that was nothing like Cameron had seen on his world. The place had seemed very cluttered to him but Jules had told him before that every thing in the room had a specific purpose and it all worked together in a way that was too complicated for him to explain. Still Jules had let Cameron watch him make the temporaries from time to time.

Cameron at first was a little afraid of them and didn't like watching them come into existence. He thought they were creepy enough as it was but to watch them be 'born' was a bit much. Then as he had gotten used to them he looked at them more as androids rather than living beings. Since he thought of them as machines, their 'birth' was now no creepier to him than watching toast pop up out of a toaster.

The process which bore the temporary helpers into existence

was not unlike birds hatching from eggs. Instead of eggs the beings came from large cocoons. They started out no larger than an average melon but quickly grew to the size of a large dog. Once the cocoon was ready it started to gyrate as the new being began to find its way to the top. Once there it would stretch first its fingers and then its entire hands through an opening it made. Then it would pull the cocoon down around itself much like a person taking off a sweater. The inside of the cocoon was only moderately damp and quickly dried up leaving large flakes behind which Granton would dutifully sweep away. The whole process would only take about thirty minutes or so depending on various factors such as humidity, time of day, and how tired Jules was at the time he began.

"I believe four of them ought to do this time". Jules told Cameron as he reached into what looked like a trough filled with clumps of dirt and moss.

"Four?" wondered Cameron. "Are you sure I'll need that many?"

"I know you are quite confident in the training you have received Cameron. And I must say you have exceeded my expectations in your ability to overcome the many denizens of the Unfinished Lands. But this is different."

"Different," mimicked Cameron. "How?"

"They are more devious than you can know. I fear even with your skills that you may need more help than just two of my temporaries could afford you."

Jules then began putting clumps of the dirt-moss mixture into another trough which mixed them with a white powder and then carried them down into a vat that popped out what seemed to Cam to be little dough balls. The dough balls then began to form into the cocoons and were laid out across the floor with enough room for them to spread into full size.

"Keep in mind that you shouldn't have to use my temporaries at all if you follow my strict guidelines."

"I understand sir." responded Cameron. "You don't want there to be any trouble."

"Exactly. I have not encountered the Gwerinathans in more years than I care to remember and I would like to keep that streak intact. If they should discover that you are in any way related to me they may suspect I am trying to harm them and may attack us one day while we are outside the palace."

"I'll be careful."

"Of course you will son." Jules told him. "And you'll be safe. Just remember to keep your distance and do not let them spot you. The temporaries will serve as a buffer should anything go wrong."

Several minutes later the temporary assistants had emerged from their cocoons and were ready for travel. Cameron packed a few things in a small knapsack and headed out the main door of the palace.

"Are you taking that strange little pet of yours with you?" Jules asked.

"Digby?" Of course. He loves to go with me whenever I'm outdoors. Unless you think it would be too dangerous."

"No, no. Go ahead." Jules relented. "I suppose he'll be fine. Perhaps he will be a little extra insurance that you will keep out of trouble."

With that Cameron, four temporaries and Digby set out toward the closest village of humans to the Unfinished Lands. The path that Jules had set for them was fairly direct and though it had a few typical obstacles they encountered nothing severe. Cameron had wandered through the Unfinished Lands countless times and had seen many of the creatures that lived there be swallowed whole by the ground or flung through the air by trees and even trampled by worms and bugs but as long as he stayed on paths indicated by Jules he never seemed to be in any danger himself. He also learned from Jules a sense of communication with the Unfinished Lands. It was almost as if he could reach out and talk to the rocks and trees with his mind. This instilled in Cameron a great sense of confidence that along with his training gave him a feeling of invincibility. Despite that feeling he knew that he would have to back away from conflict on this trip if need be.

Instructed to keep his distance Cameron took care to stay low once they were near enough to the Village to be spotted. On this particular day a couple of the village residents had just returned from fishing in the river. Cameron was very interested in watching their every move. At first he saw nothing out of the ordinary. He watched the two men clean the fish and start a fire in order to cook them. Occasionally another villager or two could be seen wandering back and forth between the modest homes he could see from his vantage point. He could tell that there were more homes and other types of buildings further on out of his sight. He really wanted to get a good luck at them so he looked around and found a small grouping of trees not far away that he felt he could climb in and get a better glimpse of the entire village. As he left for the trees one of the temporary assistants took Digby to the side and threw some of the white flake creatures he enjoyed a short distance in front of them. Then after Digby had eaten those he threw some more a little farther ahead. And finally he flung the rest several feet away towards the village. Digby ran after them.

The two villagers cleaning the fish thought they heard something. They both looked around. The temporaries quickly got themselves to the ground so as not to be seen. The villagers nodded to each other and the one closest got himself up from where he was seated and began moving slowly in the direction of the noise. He spotted Digby eating the flakes and moved excitedly but slowly towards him. When the creature was just within his range the villager took aim and threw a rock at its head. Digby was stunned and looked around. He saw the villager and looked up at him slowly. The villager threw another rock at the animal's head. Digby was stunned again but he didn't run. He looked again at the villager and twisted his head in an almost puzzled way. Just then the villager was close enough to him that he jumped towards him and grabbed him around the neck. He then jumped behind the beast and taking out his knife that he'd been cleaning fish with he slit its throat and then took the head clean off. Digby was no more.

From his vantage point in the tree Cameron watched the villager take Digby back to the fire. He hadn't seen the temporaries lead Digby away and by the time he got settled into the tree all he could tell was that the villager had killed some animal but he couldn't tell what it was. He saw them cut Digby apart and other villagers came around and seemed even more excited. He could tell they were happy about what they were going to be eating that night. He could also see that there were many small buildings in this village and that they didn't seem quite as savage as Jules had led him to believe. But he couldn't be sure from this distance. He had seen what looked like people just gathering together for a communal dinner. All was fairly peaceful. He decided he'd seen enough for at least this one day and climbed back down from the tree.

When he got back to the ground and made his way over to the temporaries he asked them where Digby had gone. One of them pointed to the north. Cameron's eyes followed the direction all the way to the village where all he could see were people preparing a large meal. Then it dawned on him and he quickly put two and two together. "No!" Cameron exclaimed quietly clinching his fist. "It can't be! Not Digby! What is wrong with those people? How could they do that to him? He is not an animal to be eaten. He's my pet, my friend!" Cameron began growing red with rage. He started to run toward the village but the temporaries held him back. He started fighting with them but the four of them quickly subdued him. They took him literally kicking and screaming away from the eyes and ears of the village and back into the Unfinished Lands.

By the time the temporaries had slowed down and began their end cycle of crumbling away Cameron was already home. Just a few feet away from the doors of the palace and with the sun setting he decided not to try and go back. He was too sore from fighting with the temporaries and still seething from the brutal murder of his pet.

He was beside himself and decided the only thing to do would be to retreat to his room to be alone. Once inside Jules was waiting to hear every last detail of the day's events.

Chapter 14
A Village Unprepared

The sun arose like any other morning over the Village of Idiots. The day began as if it were just another day. Villagers tended to their gardens. Children prepared for school. Shopkeepers tidied up their storefronts getting ready for another day of business. The weather was just as it was most any other day; warm, bright and cloudless. No special events were planned this day, nothing unusual was expected.

Borb Feargrinn sat up out of bed with a start. "Oh my!" he exclaimed. "I do believe I have overslept. And if I have overslept then I may very well be late for an appointment." In recent years Borb's memory began to slip a bit as it did for most men of his age. This fact, although not unnoticed by his fellow villagers, did little to change the expectations of his job performance as a tree tuner. "If I am as late in getting up as I expect, I should risk missing an appointment or two. Now where did I write down my appointments?" Borb scratched his head as he hurriedly put on his clothes. He went down to his kitchen and fixed himself toast and pramblers. Pramblers was a dish made from a root vegetable similar to a potato and goat cheese. The Village of Idiots had no goats since they weren't permitted livestock to care for and thus no goat cheese, so their particular pramblers were made with a cheese substitute made from nuts and water. It was a far cry from the toast and prambler you could get in the larger city restaurants but the villagers were used to it and Borb was no exception. "Oh dear," he said while looking in his cupboard, "I may be out of something. But as it is I cannot remember what it is I am out of."

Borb went to reach for the bread in his breadbox and found a scrap of paper with appointments scribbled on. "I knew it! I do have appointments for the day. Hmm... let's see here, yes, I am to be at Mrs. Winslow's house this morning to tune her trees. If I skip the breakfast which I seem to be missing some ingredients for anyway I could make it in time. Yes, yes I think I can just make it. A little drink of juice and I'm on my way." Borb found some juice in a mug in the cupboard behind the bread he needed for toast. After quickly drinking it down he sped off toward Mrs. Winslow's house near the northeastern edge of the village.

After a good breakfast Lyndon got into his yard clothes and headed out to his garden. He stood at the edge of the garden with his hands on his hips and looked around at the sky. "It's a fine day for gnome adjusting I'd say." Lyndon had the largest collection of gnomes in all of Gwerinatha. There were some who envied his collection like his friend Renny but most people thought he was a bit obsessed with them. He had such a large collection of gnomes that he couldn't display them all at once so he would rotate the collections like a museum might rotate exhibits. He kept most of the gnomes that weren't on display in a large shed he had built especially for them behind his house. "Now let's see here. Who's been out the longest and who needs a break?" he muttered to himself while scratching his head. "Yes, you there have been out a long time, you can go back in storage. And you. And you. And oh, yes, you too." Lyndon liked talking to his gnomes as he put them in and out of storage. While most people in the cities might find this strange Lyndon's behavior was quite normal in the Village of Idiots. In fact, he was looked up to as one of the brightest and most well respected villagers. In all it took about an hour to figure out which gnomes should be put back in the shed and which should be put out for display. Soon he had a lineup of gnomes placed on the side of his wall ready to go out for display.

"Now then, where should you be my friends?" One by one he put the gnomes out into his garden and around his front yard. Not long after he had begun his friend Renny stopped by to watch. "Good day Lyndon, adjusting gnomes again I see."

"Hello, Renny. It's nice to see you again." Lyndon said with a large smile. "Yes it is gnome adjusting time once again. You know I don't like leaving them the same for too long. Get's a little boring you see."

"Quite." said Renny.

"Today I think I shall have a warm weather theme for my gnomes. What do you say Renny?"

"Lovely idea Lyndon."

"Would you like to help then?" Lyndon inquired.

"Well I had thought about giving you a hand as long as it doesn't end up like the last time."

Renny had helped Lyndon arrange gnomes on several occasions in the past. Quite often it would end up with the two of them in an argument and Renny storming off in a huff. The most recent gnome arranging situation went just that way.

"Nonsense!" Lyndon shouted back at Renny. "You know I enjoy spending time with my best friend and favorite hobby at the same time. What could be better?"

"Well you do have a fairly particular way in which you like your gnomes arranged. I sometimes feel I don't get much say in the matter."

Lyndon stopped staring at his gnomes for just a second and looked over at Renny who was sitting on a stump. He bent his head down and with a wry smile he said, "Now, Renny, whose garden is it after all?"

"Well it's yours of course..."

"Exactly." Lyndon said folding his arms in front of his chest. "Which is why I get final say on where they go. You know I listen to your opinions dear friend but it is my house and I have to live here with all the neighbors coming by looking at my gnomes on a daily basis. Ultimately it's on me if the presentation isn't just right. I have a reputation to uphold. A standing in the community as it were."

Renny got up from the stump. "Well, maybe I'll just go."

"More nonsense Renny. You get over here right now and pick up a gnome. You get next choice as to where one should go."

"Well all right." Renny said and took a step towards the gnome lineup. He crossed his arms and put a finger to his lips as he sternly gazed up and down the colorful collection. He then turned his head and began looking at the garden. He took a few steps away from the house and began stretching his arms out and used his hands as a viewfinder. He walked around and around the house doing this for several minutes. Meanwhile Lyndon sat down on the stump and began to grow impatient.

"I haven't got all day you know. Are you going to make a selection or not?"

"Well not if you're going to hurry me like that Lyndon. You just got done explaining to me how important this silly gnome display is to you and as your good friend I think I should be allowed to take the time to want to help you do it right. Is there anything wrong with that?"

"No, no not at all." Lyndon said sheepishly. "I'm sorry to rush you, please go ahead and take your time."

Renny then went over and picked up one of the gnomes. He held it up and looked behind his back at Lyndon who was watching intently. He then turned back to the gnome and looked around for just the right spot. He walked over to the far side of the garden and began to put it down. He peeked over at Lyndon who was nodding his head back and forth. He then walked a few paces to the right and sat the gnome down and looked over for Lyndon's approval. Lyndon nodded affirmatively and the decision was made.

"Excellent Renny. See? I told you there'd be no problem with you helping me."

Lyndon then went over to the gnome that Renny had just put down and moved it two thirds of a rotation. He looked down at it and a big grin gradually grew across his face. "That's better. Don't you think Renny? Renny?"

Lyndon looked around for his friend but could not see him anywhere. He had left in a huff and was already plain out of sight.

Just then Lyndon thought he heard a noise in the distance. He wasn't sure what it was but it was unlike anything he'd heard before. He looked over to his gnomes and then looked back off in the distance toward the strange sound. He headed back to his gnomes but then the noise grew louder still so he decided to investigate.

He walked past a few houses and could better make out the noise he was hearing. Shrieks, screams, pleas for help and the slashing of sword on flesh was what he had determined the noises to be. He began walking more slowly realizing all at once as the screams grew louder that the best thing for him to do was to immediately change direction. He turned around and began running for his life. The next thing he knew he was headed toward the outskirts of the village his screams for help now added to the cacophony.

As he was running past Mrs. Winsow's house he tripped on a root and fell. Borb Feargrinn noticed this and immediately went over to help. "Lyndon! Are you all right?" asked Borb as he ran toward him.

"Get out! Run away Borb! Save yourself, it's most dreadful!"

"What?" Borb asked. "What are you talking about?"

"Can't you hear it?" Lyndon asked as he got up and began to brush himself off. "The screams Borb, the screams!"

Borb stood silent for a moment and then got wide eyed. He had been so intent on his job of tuning the trees in Mrs. Winslow's yard that he hadn't heard anything else. Now that his attention was brought to it he could hear the screams quite clearly. He could not only hear the screams, the shrieks and the pleas for help as well as the slashing of sword on flesh he could also see exactly what was causing it. He stood staring frozen in fear, mouth agape as Lyndon ran past him screaming.

Chapter 15
A Sour Wind is Blowing

As the weeks wore on the debate over the rights for hunting in Anhysbys Forest heated up once again. Past town meetings had erupted in shouting matches between those who thought humans had the right to hunt anywhere and those who believed that some parts of Gwerinatha should be left alone. There were many sides to the issue and so yet another meeting had been planned in the center of New London. Urien and some of his men were on standby in case anyone got out of hand. Seren and some of the wildlife defenders were there as they were at all the meetings to make sure their voices were heard. Samuel as usual was there to act as moderator.

Samuel entered the already crowded town hall wearing a long judicial type robe. The crowd went from a loud buzz to a soft murmur as he strode down the aisle to the podium. He looked around at the people seated in front of him, all anxious to get the events underway and began to speak. "Everyone, everyone, let us be silent so I may be heard." The crowd immediately quieted down. "I know this has been a very divisive issue of late and you all know that I feel there are far more important things to discuss. But because of the friction caused by the debate it is prudent we make a decision once and for all so that we can indeed get on to other things. Therefore we have gathered here to have a civil discussion on the merits of allowing hunting in Anhysbys Forest. After today's meeting it should be decided by committee whether the issue should be brought up for referendum so that the people themselves can make a final decision. You will all be allowed to speak, one after another keeping in mind of course that we keep our thoughts concise and to the point due to time constraints. And please of course, we ask that you be absolutely civil with one another. The government of Gwerinatha and I thank you for your cooperation in this regard."

After Samuel had finished the people were allowed to speak. Seren and the wildlife defenders argued that the deer in Anhysbys Forest were for the wolves to eat since they had been driven from their homes in Serenity Forest. Others argued that people were more important than wolves and the wolves should be destroyed anyway. There were those who expressed concern that Anhysbys Forest was too dangerous for humans to be hunting in. They were met with derision by the hunters who said they should worry for themselves and let the hunters who were brave enough go in to Anhysbys Forest. Still others pointed out the closeness of Anhysbys Forest to the Unfinished Lands and the fear that hunting there may bring unwanted attention from the creatures who lived there. There had been rumors of many fierce and powerful creatures roaming the forest from the Unfinished Lands and though they had long since been put aside as old wives' tales they had recently popped up again. Some said the rumors were just made up by the wildlife defenders who were grasping at straws to get their agenda moved forward and that the creatures hardly ever strayed from the Unfinished Lands anymore. Others said the rumors were true but the hunters would hear none of it. They spoke the loudest even though they seemed to be in the minority opinion.

Since Branwen's death the story of her garden spread throughout Gwerinatha. As it did so a feeling of sympathy for the wildlife grew there. For years even Serenity Forest was thought of as off limits for humans to hunt. But as more years passed the feeling began to fade. Hunters began to take more and more deer from Serenity Forest and soon it didn't seem to be enough. The government had planned for a moratorium on deer hunting in certain parts of the forest to give the deer time to replenish. But the hunters fought against that saying the need to feed the people was too great. A similar project to bring more deer to Hunoliaeth Forest had failed years earlier. The wildlife defenders had accused the hunters of not being patient enough while they countered with the idea that their hungry children were the reason for their impatience. As the deer became scarcer the hunters gained more support. If their momentum kept up they'd soon have the majority of the people behind them.

Hours of civil debating went by and soon the last speaker was set to begin. His name was Reece and he had long been the voice for the animals in Serenity Forest. He had a long thin face and was very tall. He had a quiet demeanor but when it came to this subject which was so very dear to him he had been known to speak in a very authoritative tone. He stood up and cleared his throat. The hunters and their supporters began to grumble prompting Samuel to adjust in his seat as if to give the impression of a father who was about to threaten punishment on his children. They seemed to get the message and quieted down but looked none to happy about it.

"As you all know," Reece began, "I have long been in favor of keeping the ban on hunting in Anhysbys Forest. Not only are there many species of animals there that could be in danger of being eradicated from our world but there is also the great danger of..."

Just then the doors of the assembly hall were thrust open as a man burst through yelling. "Everyone! Terrible! Terrible! It's awful! It's horrible!"

Everyone turned to look as Urien and a couple of his men escorted the man to the front of the room.

"What is the meaning of this interruption?" asked Reece in an agitated tone.

"Yes, Urien." added Samuel. "I do believe an explanation is owed as to why you allowed this man here in this manner."

"Indeed sir." Urien said while supporting the man who was having a hard time trying to catch his breath. "We tried to delay him but once you hear his message you will understand."

The man pulled himself away from Urien and began running around the room with his arms up in the air. "Oh, it's horrible! It's horrible!" he screamed. "They're gone! They're all gone! What have they done?"

"Could someone please restrain this man?" pleaded Samuel as the crowd began to become restless at the sight of the troubled man.

"We've tried sir." said Hayden, one of Urien's chief officers who had entered with the others. "He says his name is Borb Feargrinn. He's from the Village of Idiots and he was found roaming around the Village of Shallow Creek in much the same condition as you see here."

"Borb Feargrinn?" Samuel inquired. "I know this poor man. I haven't seen him in years but yes, I do recognize him now. He is an old friend. Borb! Listen, man, what is the trouble?" Samuel said as he reached out to him with both arms. Borb allowed Samuel to put his hands on his shoulders he then reciprocated the gesture and stared into Samuel's eyes as tears began to trickle down his colorless cheeks. "They're gone Samuel." Borb choked.

"Who is gone man? Tell us!" Samuel demanded.

"My village. Everyone in my village!" Borb answered. "We were attacked by a, a raiding party or an army or something, I, I don't know."

The crowd immediately began to stir. Some got up and shrieked while others sat still in their seats, unbelieving. Samuel gestured to everyone to sit down and listen to Borb. After a few minutes the crowd was settled and Borb was starting to calm down. Hayden stood up and took the podium.

"He is not in any condition to speak." Hayden began, "I can tell you what we know to this point. Some of my men found Borb in the Village of Shallow Creek as I have said. He was going on in this manner. I sent some of my men to the Village of Idiots to see if there was anything to his halted ramblings. They corroborated all he has said. It's all true." The crowd gasped. "The Village of Idiots was attacked. Almost everyone was killed." The crowd gasped again and a couple of the women screamed. Seren sat in stunned silence and her eyes got bigger as Hayden went on. "There were few if any survivors. I'm not sure how many at this point. The ones who were alive at the time were being tended to in Shallow Creek as we left this morning. I cannot say who was responsible. But it is far worse than anything our generation has seen from the monsters of the Unfinished Lands. I know of nothing like it even in our recorded history." "All gone!" Borb screamed from the corner where he had been silent and relatively calm for the last several minutes. Hayden turned at the sound and then turned back to the crowd. "I believe whoever did this let Borb go to tell of the horrendous deed.

"Preposterous!" an older man from the crowd yelled out. "The creatures of the Unfinished Lands would not be capable of such a vile atrocity."

"Nevertheless..." spoke up Urien, "...here we are. If they are not behind this then who could it possibly have been?"

"Wild animals form the forests!" a hunter yelled out.

"You're barmy!" yelled a man from the wildlife defender's group. "Animals wouldn't' possibly—"

"Hush! All of you!" Samuel cautioned. "We have to get hold of ourselves. We must learn exactly what happened and why if we are to prevent it from happening again." He couldn't help but look over at Seren who stared at him and nodded her head back and forth as if in denial.

"It wasn't forest animals that did this." Hayden responded. "From what bits of ramblings we could make sense of from Borb and from the clues left in the village it seems that men were mostly involved." More gasping from the crowd went forth. "Men, or something closely akin to them. They had crude weapons. But it was easy to see that most of the villagers died from blows to the head by blunt objects and some were obviously killed by sharp weapons such as axes or swords."

"Swords?" someone yelled. "What are we going to do?!" someone else yelled. The entire crowd began to scream out questions and demand answers at the same time.

Samuel had begun his day worried about a debate on an issue that he had felt a lower priority. He had wished that something would happen to let the people see how the government should be using its time on more pressing issues. He hadn't intended on that something inducing panic however.

***

Deep in Anhysbys Forest as Sophie and her younger litter mates were out playing they came across the portal key lying on the ground. "What's this, Sophie?" her younger brother said.

"Here now, let me see that."

Sophie examined it closely. "I have no idea what it is but we had better take this to father. He'll know what to do with it."

Sophie and her siblings did just that and Louie having a vague memory of seeing the portal key long ago thought it must be important. "I know this looks familiar to me Sophie but I can't quite place what it is exactly. Wait for it... That's it! A key! It's the key that my friend Robert used to get to Gwerinatha! This is amazing!"

"What should we do with it father?"

"I'll take it to Branwen's Garden and see if any of her sisters are there. Samuel will want to have it I'm sure."

Just before they got to Serenity Forest Louie and his family were surprised by a nghuryll. Having not eaten in a while it was a particularly nasty nghuryll at that. Since wolves are much faster and more agile than nghurylls, they had little trouble chasing the hungry creature away but the short melee did not go unnoticed. A shot rang out in the distance. Louie looked up and saw a hunter from the western most village coming toward them. He had his family well trained for such an occurrence and they scattered quickly but in so doing lost track of the portal key.

When the hunter got close enough to where Louie's family scared off the nghruyll he saw the key and picked it up. He looked at it intently for a moment and then put it in his pocket and walked away.

Chapter 16
Attack Plans

In Gule's war room a large map of Gwerinatha filled the room on a central table. Overseeing the map was Gule on one side of the table and Granton on the other. Both seemed in a jovial mood. Granton was scratching out an area on the map just north of the Unfinished Lands. "Good, good!" said Gule in a quiet yet excited tone. "The first stage in our plan to eradicate the humans is complete. The Village of Idiots, so aptly named, is no more. They were an easy conquest to be sure but each step brings us closer to our ultimate goal of human elimination."

"What is next sir?" asked Granton finishing his scratching of the Village of Idiots off the map. "The humans in other villages will be on their guard now. Do you think they may build a force to combat your own?"

"If they do it will be too late Granton." replied Gule. "You see they are divided at the moment. I had counted on that. The seeds of discontent were sown before I left and from what my sources tell me they have matured into disarray. They are having a difficult enough time agreeing on simple things. By the time they find out the need to put together an army to attack my own their numbers will be insignificant." Gule sat back in his chair and fell into a deep thought. Granton watched patiently from the other side of the table motionless. A slow smile began to move from one side of Gule's small crooked lipless mouth to the other. "The timing could not have been more perfect." He slowly stood up and walked around the table and then pointed to a spot on the map. "The next step, Granton, is Hollow Creek, the next village in line. They will think we are moving in an orderly fashion based on simple geography after this attack and then of course I will change the game altogether."

Outside the palace Cameron had been pacing the grounds. He was troubled. He kicked around rocks, broke twigs and ripped weeds from the dirt. He then slumped to the ground and put his head in his hands. His mind was tormented. He had never killed a man before let alone a score of them. Yet here he had returned from a battle in which he and an army of misanthropic creatures and temporary men had wiped out an entire village of people. There weren't just men either. Women and children suffered the same fate. Although Cameron was told these were not people in the sense that he knew them he still felt uneasy. His anger over the loss of his pet could only take him so far.

It had in fact been the straw that broke the camel's back. He was never an outcast but he wasn't particularly gregarious either. He wasn't a bully but he did have a chip on his shoulder that kept him from making many friends. He hadn't started out as a loner but he had become one during his days in Gwerinatha. And now he was a killer. He was now a warrior in Gule's army to eliminate humans. Was this his destiny he wondered? Having had no great purpose in his life before he felt a strange sense of satisfaction in what he had done. But now the rage that had kept him going during the battle had turned to guilt which led to depression. Angry and confused he decided to confront Jules another time about the path of destruction he was heading down.

Cameron searched all throughout the palace until he finally found Jules and Granton just outside a room not far from where the temporaries were made. "Ah Cameron!" exclaimed Jules. Jules had gotten used to having to change his form from Gule whenever Cameron approached. Despite that he still preferred remaining his natural self and lately he had been staying in his Jules form more often just to keep from going through the uncomfortable process too much. "We have been expecting you. The brave warrior returned from victory!"

"That's what I've come to talk about sir." Cameron began slowly. "You see, I ..."

"It's all right." Jules said as he put a quieting finger to Cameron's lips. "I understand." Jules put his arm around him as he escorted him into the room. "You mean to tell me that you are not deserving of the moniker." Cameron tried to interrupt but Jules went on. "You do not have to tell me that you did not feel very brave. I know." he said putting his free hand to his chest. "I can only imagine how it must have felt that first time into battle. You would have been a fool if you had felt no fear whatsoever. It is no reason for shame."

"Well, it's not so much that..." Cam began again only to be shot down once more.

"Listen to me, Cameron. A warrior does not speak of these things. I trained you in all the physical forms of battle you would need to survive in this world. But I see you need more. That is why I have brought you here into the armory." Jules waved his arm around the room and Cameron's eyes followed. His excitement over seeing the armor and weapons that filled the room momentarily pushed any depression out of his mind. Jules picked up different swords and had Cameron hold each of them until he found one that was just right. Some of the swords seemed to glow with an internal light. The one Cam settled on was a broadsword with a dim purple glow. Then he showed him battle armor and had him try it on. The style was like nothing Cameron had exactly seen before. If Cameron had paid a little more attention in his history class he might have thought the armor resembled that of several different cultures mixed together. It fit him perfectly. The shining armor was gold in color but it didn't feel heavy or awkward at all. In fact it felt energizing to Cameron. It was as if he had plugged into a battery when he put it on. His excitement grew with each piece of armor that Granton helped Jules put on him. When he was completely fitted he picked up his sword and spun around the room thrusting it high into the air.

"That's it Cameron," remarked Jules glancing at Granton with a wry smile. "That's a warrior born! You were made for this armor." Jules stood for a moment with his arms crossed as Cameron admired himself in a long mirror. "And let me tell you why I am giving you this now." Jules stepped closer to Cameron and put his hand on his shoulder. He then looked into the mirror at Cameron and continued. "The first battle was but a skirmish. Those beasts had no knowledge of the ways of war and no civilized weaponry. From here on out you will be faced with more serious challenges." Cameron stared intently into Jules' reflection as he went on. "Yes, the rest of the beastly sub humans you will fight will be armed. But you have nothing to fear with this armor on. It will protect you from their strongest weaponry. And you should also be aware that some of them even have abilities far beyond other men. Abilities they acquired from stealing my people's technology. But fear not for this armor takes that into consideration as well. All you have to do is remember my training and all will be well." Jules and Cameron then turned to look at each other face to face. Jules smile increased. "You will not fail."

A glazed look came over Cameron. He had forgotten his meaning for speaking with Jules in the first place. There was an eagerness to try out his new toys on the field of battle. A fresh excitement filled him up. "What's next?" Cam asked.

"The Village of Hollow Creek." Jules said flatly. I have a new crew of creatures coming in tonight. By the morning I'll have thirty or so temporary soldiers ready for battle and you will have my plans for attack. And by tomorrow evening there will be one less village of our enemies."

Cameron looked down the end of his sword as he held it up. He started intently at it while a grin forced its way onto his face. He turned to Jules while still holding the sword out and his grin was reflected back at him. "I'm ready." he said. "Whenever and wherever."

Chapter 17
A New Worry

Most people in New London were going about their daily affairs as they did any other day. The news of the raid on the Village of Idiots had simmered down somewhat over time. Many thought it wasn't as much to worry about since it was so far to the south. Others weren't as worried because they knew that many of the Southern Guard, which had been absorbed into the Gwerinathan Guard, were the best fighting force imaginable and could handle the situation. Still some weren't so sure and were preparing for the worst. There were still rumblings and grumblings among the crowds that shopped and worked in the city. But on this particular day the rumblings and grumblings seemed to pick up a little more steam. The crowds in the center of town began to get a little larger and louder than usual bordering on a disturbance of the peace.

In his office, Samuel was going over some paper work when he could no longer ignore the noise. He got out of his chair and as fast as his incredibly old frame would allow opened the door of his office to see his aide, Steffan, gone from his chair. He looked around to find Steffan at the front door watching with great anticipation the events outside. "Here now, Steffan!" Samuel remarked, "What is going on that has created such a stir amongst the people and has kept you away from your work?"

"Pardon me, sir. That is just what I am trying to find out." Steffan replied barely turning his head to acknowledge Samuel's presence.

"Let me see now." Samuel said as he inched his way past Steffan out the front door.

Samuel could see that the crowd was much larger than usual for this time of day. It was still mid-morning and the crowd was twice the size of the lunch rush. He could see that most were gathered in one place trying to hear someone speak. But the noise was so much with everyone talking and shouting that people were having difficulty hearing. Some people he could see off to the sides moaning and sobbing. A few were even running around in circles wringing their hands. Samuel addressed one such person as they ran by.

"Here now, sir. What is causing all this commotion?"

"Another attack!" the man screamed. "There's been another attack! Another village has been laid waste by the vile creatures of the Unfinished Lands! It's horrible, horrible! We're all surely doomed!"

"Seeing as this is only Tuesday," Samuel began as he looked back toward Steffan, "I'm afraid this has the makings of an incredibly trying week."

"What are we to do sir?" asked Steffan as he and Samuel went back into their offices.

"We wait for the moment, Steffan. The governor will be here soon enough expressing his concern. At that time we shall began the conversation of what to do. For the moment we just need to pray everyone is safe and that the security forces can keep any riots from breaking out."

Only three minutes passed before Governor Wellington, the man elected after the passing of Governor Baylies, entered through the door. "Samuel!" he screamed. "We have to do something; the whole of Gwerinatha is in a panic!"

"What took you so long Barclay? I would have thought you'd have been here before now." Samuel said looking at an amused Steffan.

"What? What are you talking about man? Can't you see what's going on? There is panic in the streets. And it's not just here; it's all over the land. We have to do something and we have to do it now!"

"And what are you expecting *me* to do?" asked Samuel. "How long have you been governor now Barclay? Have you no sense of when to hold a counsel meeting. Do you expect that I must do your job for you?"

"I do not have the time or patience for this now Samuel. Just look out the window. Things are out of control."

"Exactly." Samuel said reaching up to governor Wellington. He put his hand over the governor's shoulder. "You have to regain control. You have to have composure. If the people see you in a panic it will only get worse for everybody."

"You're right of course. Samuel. But what do we do?"

Samuel sighed. Since he had come out of seclusion the people had looked to him as their leader. Even though Governor Baylies had been in power for a while, at the time of Samuel's reappearance he still was looked at as mostly a figurehead by the people at large. The relatively newly elected Barclay Wellington had even less of an imprint since he had so little experience. Samuel had spent much of his time trying to give governor Wellington the confidence he needed to believe in himself as the true leader of Gwerinatha. Despite many efforts whenever things got tough the governor would always come running to Samuel. This time was no different in that respect but even Samuel realized that there was little hope in getting Barclay up to the task of taking an authoritative role in what seemed the greatest crisis Gwerinatha had ever known.

"Steffan!" Samuel cried.

"Yes sir." Steffan replied rushing out of his office.

"Get me Urien at once. Have him bring anyone who has any knowledge of these attacks with him."

"Yes, sir. Right away." Steffan replied and then quickly took off through the front door.

Samuel looked at governor Wellington who was now sitting across from him in his guest chair, head in his hands and rocking slowly back and forth. "We will have a meeting soon enough Barclay. We will find out everything we possibly can about what has happened. And then we will determine a course of action."

"Oh thank you Samuel, thank you." The governor said as he stood up to leave.

"And Barclay..."

"Yes Samuel?"

"Please try and keep a level head. Do not show the people the fear and confusion you have shown me in this room. If you cannot have it in you to do this then I suggest you at the very least *act* as if you do.

"Yes Samuel. Of course."

The governor then straightened his collar, cleared his throat, lifted his head and marched through the front door. Samuel could hear the crowd rushing over to see the governor and barrage him with questions. He would have walked the governor out himself but he did not want to take the attention away from him.

Later that afternoon the governor, Samuel and Urien met with the Gwerinathan Guard who were witnesses to the results of the latest attack. As they feared the story was every bit the same as the Village of Idiots attack. The only difference being the attacking army seemed larger this time and had defeated some of the guard as well as civilians.

There had never been a need for an army in Gwerinatha before and there was no military training as such. The men were mostly trained as officers of the peace and were mainly hunters and farmers by day. But now they had to become a fighting force. Samuel made that reluctant determination and named Urien the general of what now was to be an army. Their next step they decided was to enlist and train as many able bodied men who could help them. In the meantime they would try and get as many men as possible to the south. If the attacking force was to continue down the side of the mountains they reasoned Dyffryn Heul would be their next target and they had to be prepared.

Chapter 18
Another Town Bites the Dust

Early in the morning in Dyffryn Heul the sun had begun to rise. The misty sunrises in this city near the hot springs are one of its main attractions for holiday goers. This particular morning there were no sightseers taking in the lovely view. The sunrise looked as it does most any other day but this was not holiday season and so the town was not as crowded. More importantly, word had gotten to the people who live here, mostly employees in the hospitality industry, to take precautions against a possible attack. Everyone was already quite aware of the previous attacks on nearby villages and many had evacuated to other towns. The few people remaining had locked themselves in good and tight.

Cameron noticed the sunrise as he led his army over the hill that gave him his first glimpse of the beautiful resort town. He took a deep breath of the fresh air and looked intently into the sun slowly rising through the mist. "What a great day to rid the world of disease my friends. I think we may even have a little fun today."

The comments were completely ignored by the two figures standing closest to him. Seven Eighty Four and Seven Eighty Five were the names he had given to his current companions. It no longer bothered him that they never answered back. He had long since gotten used to their being mute and their lack of emotions. In order to give them a little more character he had taken to given them different colored bandanas that he would wrap around their head, arms or legs. This also helped to differentiate them when the need arose. Later, after they would crumble to dust he would gather the bandanas and reuse them on the next crew of temporary men Jules would make for him.

Cameron and his two lieutenants, as he liked to refer to them during attacks, surveyed the area and began devising a plan. "Seven Eighty Five, you will take your men down toward the springs. Seven Eighty Four, you will take your men to the opposite side and I will take the rest straight up the middle. Your orders are straightforward. Torch the buildings and kill any and everyone who rushes out." Cameron looked behind him and made sure that his army was ready. There were still a few stragglers coming up the hill. They were the more cumbersome creatures from the Unfinished Lands. Some of them could not move very quickly but they were very strong and were very efficient in killing people in hand-to-hand combat. Cam himself preferred to work mainly with temporaries because they didn't slow him down so he took a score of them with him down the middle path toward the center of Dyffryn Heul.

There was no yell of 'charge' or a stampede toward the town. Instead the army marched down in relative quietness and proceeded with a slow and orderly process of throwing torches onto the roofs of the buildings. Dyffryn Heul was made up mostly of cottages with charming thatched roofs that fit in well with the climate and the look and feel of a romantic getaway destination. They also caught fire rather quickly which suited the methodical pace of Cameron's advancing hoards.

Soon most of the buildings were ablaze and Cameron looked around with a look of disappointment on his face. "I can't believe there's nobody here. I don't hear any screaming or whimpering or anything." He then shouted so that anyone might hear over the crackling flames. "Are you people going to rob me of the pleasures taken in killing you scum?" After a moment or two with no answer he shouted again. "Oh c'mon, you guys. Surely there's somebody left hiding in this stupid place. Do you all want to die of smoke inhalation? Aren't there any of you brave enough to come out here and get killed by my sword? I bet you weren't a bunch of little sniveling snots when you tortured the real humans that lived here! You're all a bunch of weak punks!" Then he turned to his mute soldiers and shrugged his shoulders at them. "What a waste of time this is!"

At that moment a shriek came from behind Cameron as a man burst through the flames with a pitchfork. He ran directly at Cameron who swung around just in time to slash through the man's middle. The man dropped the pitchfork and stared up at Cameron, his eyes bulged and blood began to ooze from his gaping jaw. He fell at Cameron's feet onto the dusty ground. Noticing the man's clothes were still on fire, Cameron kicked him over on his back and put out the flames. "Just a lesson, people. This is what can happen if you don't stop, drop, and roll!"

Cameron looked around and saw a few more people starting to come out of the burning edifices. Each was taken out quickly by a temporary or a creature wielding a club, axe, spear or sword. "Now this is more like it. At least the day will not be a total loss."

After a few more minutes there wasn't a building left that hadn't succumbed to the raging inferno. The shrieks from inside the buildings were getting fewer and farther between like the popping of popcorn kernels in the microwave Cameron thought. He figured everything was about over when a rumbling sound came from the west. At first he hadn't noticed it over the noise of cracking timbers and collapsing roofs but then it became impossible to ignore. He looked in the direction of the noise and saw a few dozen horses and riders coming towards him. It looked as though they were shooting at Cameron's army. Once they got a little closer he could see that was indeed the case. Some of the creatures in his army started falling to the ground. Cameron took a defensive position and began to beam. "Now this is going to get exciting after all."

As the horses got nearer Cameron could see they did not look like the ones he was familiar with at all. "What the heck kind of horses are those?" he said while watching one of them tear a temporary in two pieces with its talons. "Oh man, I have got to get me one of those!" In his distracted state he let his guard down long enough to get into firing range of one of the riders. Cameron felt a sharp pain as if someone had hit him in the gut and he realized he'd been shot in the chest but the tiny bullet bounced off his armor. Irritated, Cameron ran at the shooter. Now much closer in range the rider took aim and shot Cameron again. This time the bullet glancing off his helmet. "Ow! That hit me in my head! You're in for it now dude!" Cameron jumped into the air and slashed at the rider causing him to fall off his horse. He then ran over to the man who was still armed and stomped on his gun hand. "Oh no you don't!" Cameron yelled before stabbing the man in the throat. He then pulled his blade back just in time to defend himself from another armed guard. "You people don't know when to quit do ya? Well that's all right with me. This is better than I had hoped for!"

On through the morning the battle raged. The mist long ago evaporated by the rising sun and heat from the fires made every ghastly sight visible to everyone. At times three and four temporaries were able to take down a horse and then overcome the rider. Some of the larger creatures were invulnerable to bullets as their hides were so craggy and tough. They plodded their way through the advancing guard with relative ease. The guards from the west though armed with pistols were outnumbered significantly by Cameron's army. They had taken out far more of his creatures and temporaries than Cameron expected with their guns. But even though they were causing Cam's army to shrink faster than their own they reached a point where they were down to only five men left against a good two dozen or so. The five men managed to get their horses close enough together to make a hasty retreat back toward the mountains and on to the north lands. "That's it, run!" Cameron yelled at them. "Run, but it won't be long before I come for you too! It's only a matter of time before I rid this place of all you scum!"

Cam looked around at the corpses, some blackened by the fire. He saw many more of his men dead than ever before. He noticed the temporaries that survived were beginning to gray out. "All right! We're done here! Let's move out!" he shouted. "It won't be long before it's just me and you creeps. The temps won't make it back with us from this range. We've spent too much time here today. But we had fun didn't we?" A few groans and nods came from his audience of Unfinished Land denizens. They were weary and though they were coming closer to their goal of ridding themselves of their enemy they didn't seem to share the excitement that Cameron had. They were reluctant to make him into their hero as to them he represented the enemy. They tolerated him because he was accomplishing what they could not on their own, but there would be no carrying him on their shoulders or great cheers of victory.

Cameron ordered a few of the temporaries to try and corral one of the horses for him. He walked up to it and grabbed the bridle. Staring at its beak he nodded his head. "Man, this is really cool." The horse reared back and fought against Cam. "Don't worry, buddy. I'm not gonna hurt you. I want you to be my new friend." Cam mounted the horse as two of the temps tried to hold it still. He struggled with the reins until he finally got the horse quieted. "Wow! Look at those feet. I bet they can put a nasty scratch on you. Oh, sorry Seven Eighty, guess you already knew that." Cam had wished for a second that he could've gotten a response from the temporary with a large gash across his chest but then shrugged it off and switched his attention back to his army. "Okay, this is it guys, we're headed home. Yehaw!" Cam then held on as the horse reared back on its hind legs and managed to ride it all the way back to the castle.

Chapter 19
We Need Some Heroes

When word got back to New London from the five survivors of the attack on Dyffryn Heul crowds began to panic again. Even more people than last time began to pack their things and head north. More sobbing and shrieking was heard in the streets. The crowds were so bad they compelled the governor to make an impassioned plea for calm. For the most part his words fell on deaf ears. Gwerinatha's citizens had never been through anything like this before. At most they had only seen a band of five or six creatures together causing havoc and that was usually so far away from the larger cities that no one this far north had given it much thought. But this was far different. The creatures were organized and had a human leader. They had weapons and seemed to be making a path through the southern part of Gwerinatha village by village with the sole intent of human destruction. What's worse is that now the people had fought back and they had lost. Another town hall meeting was hastily put together to try and calm the nerves of those who had not evacuated the city.

The scene was not much unlike that of the previous meeting. Samuel, the governor, and Urien stood in front of the crowd and tried to calm them for several minutes with no luck. No one wanted to listen. They just kept yelling over each other and it seemed like there would be nothing but more panic to come from the meeting. Then finally Seren, who had had enough and was about to leave, threw her hands up in the air. "This is ridiculous!" she screamed. "I know everyone's frightened but these people won't calm down long enough for anything." Then she remembered how her youngest sister used to get attention when she thought she wasn't getting any. Many times when she was younger and her older sisters would seem to ignore her, Charity Baylies would scream at the top of her lungs with such a high pitched squeal that it would cause her sisters to want to throttle her. Seren could never scream that loud but she reached behind her to where her sister was seated and told her to shriek for all she was worth.

Charity stood on top of her chair and gladly obliged. In an

instant the hall quieted down with every single face turned towards her. She sat there beaming as she hadn't realized she could still scream that loud. Her large smile only confused the few people who had rushed to her thinking she was in pain. A few others ran to the door thinking they were under attack. But she had accomplished the task Seren requested and Samuel was able to get the floor. "Thank you my dear," Samuel said addressing Charity. "Now if we could all please direct our attention this way I'd like to get this meeting started."

"The first thing I want to do is separate fact from fiction. There are enough worries going on right now without exacerbating them with unsubstantiated rumors flowing about. New London itself is not under attack and has not been. We have seen no creatures armed or unarmed lurking about our streets. I've also heard rumors that all the villages to the south of the mountains have been destroyed. Let me assure you that this is also not true." A few murmurings began in the crowd. Charity turned and stared one of the loud people down. The threat of her screaming again was enough to keep them in line. Samuel continued.

"It is true unfortunately that the city of Dyffryn Heul has been destroyed." The crowd reacted with a rather uncomfortably silent murmur that even Charity didn't attempt to stop. "Now let it be known that a good many people were able to evacuate before the city was attacked. Word got through to them in time for that but unfortunately our men did not arrive in time to save the town from being burnt to the ground. Many lives were lost and only these five men from our guard survived." Samuel had each of the men speak to the crowd to describe exactly what had taken place. It took some time as the crowd jostled and became more and more agitated as each survivor began to tell his story. By the time the last one spoke the murmurings grew to rumblings once again. Charity got up on top of her chair once more and the crowd grew quieter. Samuel took questions from them but there were very few answers to be given.

Samuel let them know that they were working as hard as they could to manufacture more guns and even some armor for their new army but since the need had never arisen before it was going to take time. The crowd feared they would not have very much time left. Samuel entertained suggestions but no one had any practical solutions until Seren spoke up about the orbs of power. Samuel looked as if he wished she hadn't mentioned that and then the crowd stirred again. The idea of letting the soldiers use the power of the orbs became very popular. And so it was decided that every remaining soldier would be bathed in the light of the green orb to increase their strength, stamina and speed. The officers would also be bathed in the light of the red orb to give them limited mental abilities. This idea certainly calmed the crowd a good bit but it had worried Samuel.

Seren had seen Samuel's face and approached him after the meeting. "What's wrong Samuel?" she asked. "Don't you think the orbs will help us? Isn't that what they were hidden for anyway, an emergency? This is certainly an emergency I would say."

"No doubt my child." Samuel answered. "This is the worst emergency I can imagine and as such I believe the use of the orbs may have to be initiated even if they fail us."

"Fail us?" she echoed. "What do you mean?"

"I do not trust the power of the orbs Seren. I hadn't meant to worry anyone but I have wrestled with the thought myself. You see the orbs were old magic, if they were ever magic at all, years ago when they were used against your sister, Branwen. I remember how powerful they were when the Originators first gave them to us. They were incredible indeed, far more powerful than they were several years ago. That is why everyone made such a fuss over them. But I have gone to check on them a time or two in the years since hiding them. The light form the orbs has faded. I fear the power within them may be waning as well. But you are right, we have to try. We have to give my people every chance we can against this danger."

Samuel sent Urien to fetch the blue orb from its hiding place in Baylies Crossing. He had sent Steffan to retrieve the red orb from its hiding place on a farm just outside New London. Then he himself went after the green orb which was being looked after by an old friend at a livery stable in New London.

Samuel went alone to make sure that no one knew just where all the hiding places were. He had thought to himself that may no longer be necessary if it turned out the orbs had lost too much power. A young man with bright red hair met Samuel at the door. "Can I help you sir?" the man asked looking up at Samuel. "Oh, oh it's you sir. Come right in."

Samuel was still bothered by his legendary status and how it affected people in the way they treated him. "Thank you, lad." Samuel replied. "You don't have to bow you know. I need to see your stable's manager. Alone."

"Yes, sir. Right away sir. I'll get him at once."

The young man ran out the door and a few minutes went by and a mule came walking through the door.

"I'm the manager. You wanted to see me?" said a voice from the left side of the mule's two mouths.

Standing in shadows Samuel was not clearly visible to his old friend Gefell. "It is I, Samuel, old friend."

"Well, so it is" the right mouth said. "So it is." Gefell walked up to Samuel and lowered his head as Samuel rubbed his neck and ears as a greeting. "It is so very nice to see you again." the left mouth said.

"Of course you haven't been by in weeks." the right mouth added.

"I am afraid this is not a pleasure call friend Gefell."

"And I was afraid you might say that." Gefell's left mouth replied.

"I did wonder why you were here without so much as a moment's notice." the right mouth added.

"I've come for the orb Gefell."

"Oh dear." the left mouth said. "The orb. The green orb. You've come to wrest it from its hiding after all this time. Something truly terrible must be going on."

"This must be why all the horses have been in such a sorry state these last few days." his right mouth added.

Gefell had been the manager of the livery stable for several years now. It was his ability to communicate with both the horses and the humans that won him the job. Since working there his nerves had calmed plenty from his days of adventuring in the Unfinished Lands. Only once in a rare while did his two voices ever get off the same page and not once in the last few years.

"Yes, Gefell. I imagine you've heard quite a lot from the horses about the panic that has gone through the city. Gwerinatha is suffering great hardships at the hands of the grotesque creatures from the Unfinished Lands. We need more help than human power alone can give."

"Oh, I knew it I knew it I knew it." Gefell's left mouth said. "I just knew there was trouble brewing."

"Stupid horses!" chimed Gefell's right mouth. "They don't know what they're talking about! Trouble from the Unfinished Lands they said. Humans and monsters attacking villages they said! People dying everywhere! Panic in the streets!"

"I am afraid it is all so very true Gefell. That is why I have come for the green orb and have even sent my men for the other two as well."

"Are we going to be attacked Samuel?" Gefell's right mouth asked.

"I cannot say."

"Are we safe here in the city?" Gefell's left mouth queried.

"I can only pray that we are at this point dear friend. New London is too large a city to evacuate quickly and frankly I do not know that any place would ultimately be safe from this threat. We need that orb."

"Yes, at once!" Gefell's left mouth said as he went to the back of one of the stalls and uncovered a secret panel with his nose. Behind the panel was a hole in the floor with an old wooden box. Samuel reached down and picked the orb out of the box. He lifted the steel sphere gently and placed it on the ledge of the stall. He slowly moved a sliding door on the sphere to reveal the green light from inside the orb.

"Well, it is still working I suppose." he muttered to himself. "But as I feared the light is not as bright as when last I saw it."

"What's that you're saying?" Gefell's left mouth asked.

"Did you say something?" his right mouth added.

"No, Gefell." Samuel replied. "Do not worry. We have hope and that is that."

"Why do I feel like you are keeping something from me Samuel?"

"Just take care of your business my friend and let us know if you hear of anything odd from the horses. We will give you as much time as possible to evacuate should the situation call for it."

Samuel then left while Gefell sat in the shadows and began to worry.

Before Steffan and Urien could arrive with the other two orbs Samuel began bathing soldiers in the green light. The orb's power was still functional and the soldiers did experience an increase in strength, stamina and agility. Fearing the next attack was imminent Samuel sent the men south of the mountains to beef up security in the City of Wellington. It was believed that city would be attacked next based on the fact that the opposing armies had been moving methodically to the east.

While Samuel's men headed to Wellington, Cameron and his armies attacked the Village of Shallow Creek just to the north of the mountains. While there was some resistance, the bulk of the Gwerinathan forces were to the south. The village was razed in a matter of hours. And as soon as the attack was finished, Cameron and his troops left for the Unfinished Lands, graying temp men crumbling as they went.

Chapter 20
Something's Missing

After the attack on Shallow Creek Cameron headed up to his room in the palace while the creatures of his army dispersed to their homes in the caves, bogs and woods of the Unfinished Lands. He sat silently for a while and did not come out of his room even when Granton notified him that his dinner had been prepared. Granton came downstairs and entered the dining area.

"He will not come down my lord." Granton told Gule. "He seems disturbed by something and of course he will not speak to me."

"And that is of course perfectly acceptable to you is it not Granton."

"Of course, my lord. I have not hid from you my distaste for the young man, only from him. He is human after all."

"So all the better for me as well Granton." said Gule wriggling in his seat. "This 'Jules' disguise is all too uncomfortable after a while and the less I have to use it the better." Gule then began to eat. He stirred bluish goo around in a bowl and looked up towards the ceiling. "Still, I cannot help but wonder what is troubling him so. He has been very good about expressing his feelings with me since he opened up to me before the invasions began."

He stirred the blue food around a little more and then began to take a few bites. He then took a few bites of a leafy green salad and began to think out loud again. "You know I do not believe he is having conscience issues with the attacks again as he did at first. I feel very confident in my persuasive powers. No, that can't be it. He has gotten to the point where he is enjoying the destruction almost as much as I am vicariously though him. If he only knew..."

"Why does it disturb you so master Gule? Surely we are far enough along in the plan that his necessity is lessening."

"Not so, Granton, not so. Though we have indeed destroyed several villages now we have only scratched the surface of the population. Most of the people live within the larger cities further to the east. We have only struck one village in the north and that is where more than sixty percent of the people live. No Granton, Cameron is still very much needed. The fear that we spread now is absolutely essential to our plans if we are to destroy the larger cities. Trust me when I tell you that when the time comes Cameron will be dealt with in the same manner as the other humans. We will be rid of every last one of them. Have patience. This is a very time consuming project." Gule began to look tired.

"It is also a very energy consuming project. Oh, if only my fellow Originators had only agreed with my assessment of the humans from the beginning. I would not be stretching myself so thinly here in this time and place. But I cannot spend my valuable energy on regrets. I must know what troubles young Cameron so that he will not lose his effectiveness on the battlefield. I am also too tired for games. I will try the more direct approach. After dinner send him to me in the war room. Let him know that his presence is demanded should he give you any resistance."

"Yes, my lord."

Granton did as Gule commanded and after a bit of persuasion Cameron was convinced that he needed to see Jules in the war room. Once he got there he could see Jules sitting in his throne leaning back with his head resting against a pointed finger and a concerned look on his face.

Cameron walked slowly toward him. "You wanted to see me?"

"Yes, Cameron. You didn't come down for dinner. I am sure you must be hungry after the battle and as you are no doubt aware there are no places to stop for food on the way home." Cameron didn't smile even though he realized Jules was attempting a joke.

"Something's troubling you isn't it lad?" Jules motioned towards the seat to his left. "Sit here and tell me about it."

Cameron looked disgusted and turned as if to walk out the door and then spun back around. Raising his hands in a frustrated gesture he walked to the seat next to Jules. "That's just it Jules!" he said in a deflated tone. "I am not a 'lad' any more. I mean I know you may always think of me as your son but I wasn't even a child when you found me and that was a dozen years ago."

"All right." Jules responded in a subdued manner. "I understand you are not a youth any more. You have certainly proved your manhood on the battlefield many times over."

Jules noticed Cameron flinch at the word 'manhood'. He saw a look of irritation overtake his face. "This something that is bothering you..." said Jules. "Might it have to do with being an adult in some way other than title or accomplishments?"

Cameron squirmed in his seat. "I don't really want to talk about this, Jules. If I did I would have come down to dinner. Yes, something's been bothering me for some time but I really don't want to talk about it."

"I believe the picture is starting to come into focus now

Cameron. I understand you do not wish to speak of your trouble but I think I may be able to help."

"I really doubt it." Cameron moaned sarcastically.

"Come now, Cameron. Have I let you down before?"

"No, it's just..." Cameron looked away from Jules and out into the hall. "I really don't feel comfortable talking about this."

"You are longing for female companionship aren't you Cameron?"

"What part of 'I don't want to talk about this' are you not getting?"

"Look, Cameron. I realize this is a touchy subject to you. But it is not such an important matter where I come from."

"Well it's a pretty big deal where I come from let me tell you."

"See Cameron, you can talk about it."

"Agh!" Cameron exclaimed as he got out of the chair. "I'm going back to my room now."

"Now wait Cameron. I am not finished with this discussion you don't want to have just yet."

"Well I am!"

"Stop!" Jules yelled as he grabbed Cameron by the arm. "This is a very delicate matter but it can be tended to."

Cameron rolled his eyes, sighed and sat back down in the chair next to Jules. "You're not gonna let this go are you?"

"No. I told you I can help you and I will." Jules said with an understanding look on his face. "Now where I come from all the male female relationships were prearranged. We would be set up as you might say with each other from birth." Cameron rolled his eyes again and squirmed in his seat.

"That's really not going to help me is it?" he said in an agitated tone.

"No, Cameron. I am just giving you my background."

"Oh please, can we just stop this." Cameron pleaded.

"Do you want help or don't you?"

"What can you possibly do to help me?"

"I am giving you permission to bring back one of the Gwerinathan women to the palace. If you find one you fancy for a wife I can accept that." Jules raised his hands toward Cameron as if to stop him from speaking. "Now I know what you are going to say, that I've told you that these people are savages and are subhuman and that you couldn't possibly see yourself betrothed to one such as this. And all that is true. They are very savage. But really it is the males that are the most troublesome. They teach their children the hate that makes them subhuman. This hate sinks into a deep level in the males so much so that it can never be eradicated. But it could possibly be reversed in the females seeing as how they are not the ones forced into battle."

"What are you telling me Jules?" Cameron asked while he sat up in his chair. "Are you saying these people can be all right after all? That they can learn to be as good as you or me?"

"Listen carefully Cameron. "I am telling you that if you long for female companionship it is something that can be afforded you. That is all you need to hear. Do not trouble yourself with the 'how's' and 'whys'. You leave that to me. I am just letting you know that what you seek is still possible even amongst the subhumans of Gwerinatha.

Cameron was very confused. He had not given any thought to the fact that the people of Gwerinatha could be like him since the lengthy discussions he'd had on the subject with Jules after the first attack. He no longer felt guilty about killing the people and in fact had taken delight in the effort. Now it was put to him that he could take one of the women from Gwerinatha as a bride. This is something that he couldn't even have considered before. He struggled with the concept and pleaded with Jules for more explanation. Jules explained how with extraordinary measures and effort he could take one of the subhuman women and conform her into a fit mate for him. Jules looked long and hard into Cameron's eyes to make sure he understood exactly what could be done. He did not want Cameron to have doubts over killing the humans again. He also did not want Cameron's longing for a mate to keep him from being effective on the battlefield.

"Relax Cameron." Jules told him as he lovingly tapped him on his forearm. "Find the one you are looking for and bring her to me. I can handle the rest. She can have a room of her own here in the palace while you are away on missions. Why she will actually be better off here with us than with those deplorable beings out there. In time she will be grateful for what you have done for her. And perhaps the two of you can even begin a new family. A family raised with higher ideals and morals than could ever be thought of out there amongst the savages."

Cameron took in a deep breath and got out of his chair one final time. He looked at Jules and smiled softly. "You know, I don't know why I was afraid to talk to you about this Jules. No matter what problems I have you seem to always know just how to handle them."

"That's right my son." Jules said. "And please, don't ever forget that."

Cameron walked out of the room feeling much better about himself despite not knowing if he could possibly find a Gwerinathan girl to interest him. But it didn't matter. He now had a greater confidence in Jules than ever before and went off to his room more excited than he had been in a long while. Jules squirmed into a cocoon of light which slowly burned off to reveal his more natural form. He then stretched out his arms and legs, let out a deep breath and sat back in his throne and relaxed.

Chapter 21
Chaos Spreads

More and more men became deputized into the Gwerinathan Guard. Each man who was sent off to protect a city was bathed in the green light before going out. The orbs' light however needs to be recharged and with soldiers now spread out all over the land it was impossible to keep everyone at full strength for long periods of time. Samuel had worried about this problem as well as the overall condition of the orbs' power. Since there were so few guns to go around, the orbs' power had become a necessity. Some men were bathed in the light of the red and blue orbs in hopes of gathering intelligence. The guard had been taken by surprise with the first attacks in the north. They had no idea how or when the next attack would take place. Without fully knowing their enemy or why they were being attacked, they were at a disadvantage despite their numbers being so much larger. The plan of the enemy to spread fear throughout the land was working.

Citizens were told to prepare themselves no matter where they lived. Those families with hunters who had not joined the guard had access to guns but for the others, they were told to grab whatever they could find to use as weapons of defense. The farming communities gathered every hoe, pitchfork and plow shear they could and had women and children stand by behind the guard in case of attack. Despite the preparation panic still spread. People were not thinking as clearly as normal and no one seemed to know exactly what to do. No one knew what city would be struck next and some even scoffed at the idea that cities would be attacked saying they had only struck small villages.

Day to day life had become a struggle. The shopkeepers who decided to stay open were either inundated by customers or completely bereft of them. Large events were being cancelled. People gathered together in groups only to discuss plans for evacuation or counter attacks. Some called for level heads to try and figure out what was going on but still others called for taking the fight to the Unfinished Lands. The latter was not a popular decision and could not muster enough interest to mount an attempt. The people of Gwerinatha were at their wits end.

In the farmland just north of the Village of Shallow Creek Cameron and his group of Unfinished Land creatures were waiting. Since the decimation of the village the farms had gone untended. Cameron used the farms as a gathering place to feed his army and wait for more temporary men to be formed. Since they were now beginning attacks so far away from the palace the temporary men no longer lasted long enough to be of any use in the battles. A solution was arrived upon when Jules and Granton crafted a portable version of the machines which created the men and their cocoons. The machinery was brought forth on wagons and took days from its arrival to its setup to the first batch of temporary men. From this point the temp men would be able to aid Cameron in battles to all but the northern most Gwerinathan cities.

Once the first batch of temp men were available Cameron sent word to attack Sibridale, the next closest city to the north. Sibridale was far more populated than any of the villages Cameron's army had attacked before so they increased their number of temporary men significantly. They sent in one hundred temporary men ahead of Cameron. There was not enough weaponry for all of the temporary men so many of them picked up rocks and sticks but most just used their brute strength and agility to attack the city. The first wave of temp men sent panic throughout Sibridale. There were twenty guardsmen stationed in the outskirts of the town along with a score of volunteer fighters. They quickly got word to the town of the oncoming attack. The temp men had no defense against bullets but only a direct hit to their head would stop them. It took a while for the guard to recognize this but after several temp men with bullet holes throughout their bodies could be seen continuing their charge into the city the idea took hold. The sight of the temp men with no faces sent shock throughout the populace. Most of the people had been prepared for the gruesome visages of the Unfinished Land creatures. Stories from eyewitness accounts had long since circulated about their grotesque bodies and disfigured faces. But the temp men were menacing in a different sort of way. They were like machines with no emotion whatsoever. They knocked over wagons and carts. They ripped up and tore through anything and everything that got in their way. They overtook most of the populace and anyone who had a weapon had it ripped from them and used against them by the much quicker temp men.

Some of the guard found themselves fighting the temp men hand to hand. Their green orb power boost was a welcome sight for the citizens of Sibridale. Those who bathed in the green orb were besting the temp men in combat. Even though the temp men were far from running out of time they were unstable due to their incomplete origins. A bullet anywhere except the head would only settle into their claylike features but a strong blow such as brought on by a green orb enhanced guardsmen would send them shattering like glass. A couple of guardsmen caught on to this and they began using teamwork to smash the temp men into each other. A wave of hope rushed through the crowd as the battle waged on. Just when it looked like the tide might turn another wave of temp men came in after them.

Hour after hour the brave men and women fought back against the seemingly endless wave of temp men. Storefronts were destroyed. Fires were burning all around the town. Corpses were scattered in the streets. The guard never backed down. The initial guard that had been on the border was now down to only three men. The guard inside the city had brought reinforcements as every able bodied person in the city of Sibridale was now involved in the war. Children picked up toys and used them as weapons. Women grabbed knives from their kitchens and fought off brutal attacks by temp men invading their homes. When it seemed as if there may be hope of yet squashing the temp men a final wave of them came forth with Cameron and a score of Unfinished Land creatures alongside them.

The city of Sibridale thought it could not be any more frightened than it was. Death and destruction were everywhere. Temp men were crashing through windows and dragging screaming people into the streets and now the monsters came. The people were led kicking and yelling and pleading for their lives into the brutal hands of the gruesome attackers. The much slower creatures easily fought off the weakened citizens. The last bits of hope began to vanish like vapor. All the while Cameron relished in the destruction.

This time was different for Cameron. Gone were the smart-aleck remarks he had found himself so tempted to make in previous battles. This was serious. The stakes were higher. For the first time he and his men proved they could vanquish an entire city. Razing a village was nothing compared to this. His adrenaline flowed and he enjoyed every slash of the sword and every agonized scream of his foes. The fact that his army was now more powerful than ever only energized him further. The guard who were left tried to make their way to Cameron hoping that they could overtake him before their power from the green orb had faded. Those that did attack them found out that amazingly once they were near him their orb enhanced abilities disappeared. Jules had not only made Cameron's armor bulletproof but impervious to the orb energies as well. The news came too late for the guard whose number was now rapidly dwindling. Cameron sent back word for one more batch of temp men to be called forward. He wanted to make sure that no one in the city remained. After another hour the last batch had joined the ranks of Cameron's army and the last of the citizens of Sibridale who had not run off to the north had given up their lives and their city. Cameron's army had won. Sibridale was vanquished.

The battle over, the temp men made sweeps throughout the city searching for survivors. Those who were found were slaughtered. This was not a war for taking prisoners. The goal was the complete eradication of the enemy and the temp men were perfect for that since they were virtually soulless machinations. Something Cameron had at one time feared becoming. That thought was now buried in the back of his mind. He had other matters that needed his attention. He sent the creatures back to the farms and left the temp men to stay on in Sibridale until they expired. He then took some time to look around the town. He found a clothing store that had been ravaged. He sorted through what he could and found some clothes that were not damaged. Picking up one item after another he tossed most of them to the ground and shook his head. He took the time to actually try on several different outfits before he got something that suited him. Thinking his new look rather sharp he had his horse brought in from the farms by some of the temp men. He then sent his armor back with them. He mounted the horse and began to ride north toward New London.

Chapter 22
Time to Leave New London

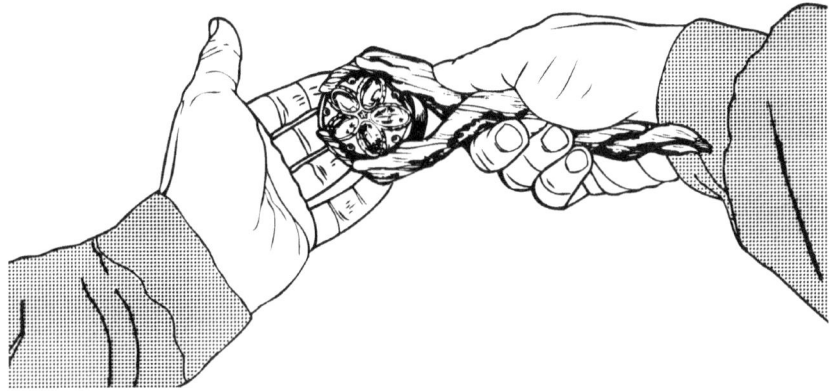

Word reached New London of the fall of Sibridale before Cameron had arrived. The city, already in panic mode, went into hysterics. People began calling for an all out evacuation of the city. They argued over where to go. Some suggested they flee to the mountains and others said everyone should move north. Being the largest city, a full scale evacuation was impractical. However many people had already left leaving many businesses understaffed.

Seren had been visiting Samuel in his office when word broke through about Sibridale. "What are we going to do Samuel?" Seren asked him. "It's only getting worse."

"I know dear, I know." he replied. "I'm afraid we are all ready doing what we can. It will take time to fashion more weapons and even more time to gather sufficient information from the enemy to be able to combat them more effectively." He paced the floor and then stopped to stare out the window. "All these people scurrying about. I feel so badly for them."

"Do they even know where they are going?" Seren asked.

"Some do. But since we do not know enough about the enemy, it's too hard to predict exactly what they will do next. So the safest place to be is still unsure." He then walked toward Seren and put his arm around her shoulder. "However we can deduce logically that they cannot yet be too far to the north and so that makes some sense as a safer destination. So many people have moved north that I am certain you will not be lonely there."

"What are you talking about?" Seren asked.

"You cannot stay here Seren. You know I have thought of you as family and I cannot allow harm to come to you."

"You think it's not safe here in the largest city?"

"Today, yes, New London is safe. But tomorrow..." his voice trailed off. He then turned and looked out the window again. "I want you to go back home to Baylies Crossing. You should be with your family at this time and I am certain you will be safer there."

"No!" I want to stay. This is my home now. I want to fight for it if it comes to that."

Samuel turned to her again and looked at her with knowing eyes. "Now Samuel I know you don't believe in women fighting but for the entire survival of the human race everybody has to fight now. Women and children are dying Samuel. You must let me at least try."

"Women and children *are* dying Seren. I don't want you to die too. Do not argue with me. Pack your most essential belongings and head to your hometown as soon as possible. I'll send word when the war is over and it is safe to return."

"Something about the way you said that Samuel." Seren said quietly. "I almost think you don't believe it."

"Nonsense girl! We must always have hope. Listen to me when I say I know that New London has the strongest defenses of all the cities in Gwerinatha. I believe we have more than a chance. It will just take the time we need to gather information and prepare the proper response. I am sure we will have enough time to do that. But in the meantime I feel it only best to send you to safety. I believe the governor will call for a mandatory evacuation of all women and children soon enough. You can be of help to the people in the north and I am sure you will be here with us in spirit. Now, go!"

Just then Steffan came into the room with a worried look on his face. "Samuel there's a man here to see you. He says it's urgent."

"Let him in then Steffan." Samuel then turned to Seren. "Go ahead, now. I'll get word to you as soon as I can." He kissed her on the forehead and she left the room.

A man brushed by her as if he didn't even see her. "Samuel! Samuel I have something for you to see!"

"Here now, what is this?" Samuel asked. "Calm down young sire and tell me what you have to say."

The man reached into his pocket and pulled out the portal key. Samuel's eyes opened widely and his jaw stiffened. "Where did you get that son?"

"I am an undertaker and this was found on a hunter who died in one of the attacks. I was sorting out his pockets and this was just there. I know what this is Samuel. I am a good friend of General Urien and I have heard all the stories of the portal key and the visitor from another world. I knew you would have to have this at once!"

"Yes, yes. You were right to bring this to me. Thank you very much." Now I'm sure you have more than enough work to do and you'd best get back to it."

"Of course sir. You're very welcome sir."

Samuel patted the man on the back as he walked him to the door all the while never taking his eyes off the portal key. He then turned and sat back at his desk fully examining the key to make sure that it was in perfect working condition.

***

Cameron rode into town with little fear of being recognized. Besides the fact that his helmet had covered much of his face he had left very few survivors in any of the attacks. He did so in order for fear to be spread among the populace. It was clear to him now that plan was working only too well. New London was such a large city if any of the survivors were still around the chances were slim Cameron would run into them. And even if he did Cameron felt certain his disguise of normal Gwerinathan clothes would keep them from guessing his identity.

With everyone running to and fro in a clear panic Cameron was able to trot through the main roads with hardly any attention paid to him at all. This suited Cameron just fine as he intended for this trip to be one of an observational nature. This wasn't just a scouting mission for future battles. His armies were almost ready to attack a city the size of New London. He had also planned to look around and see if there just might be a Gwerinathan girl that would interest him. He assumed that this being the largest city his chances would be greater here.

He had ridden around several blocks not finding a girl that quite suited him. The panic of course didn't help the situation as everyone kept running around. Still, there were a few women he had seen sitting on benches or staring out windows that caught his eye. But none of them seemed quite right. He had almost given up. He went back to thinking that these people really were subhuman and that the whole idea was futile. He had wished that Jules had never pressed him on the issue. Then he saw her. Slowly walking down the street while everyone else seemed in such a hurry Seren stood out from the others. He slowed his horse's gait so he would not overtake her. Her long wavy brown hair immediately made an impression on him. The closer he got the more attractive she seemed to him. He slowed down even more as their eyes met. He could tell her eyes were a deep blue. She seemed more startled than scared and did not run away. She just stared back at him as if she knew there was something different about him. He stopped the horse just a few feet from her and she didn't flinch.

Cameron thought back to when he and his friend Robert Moore were kids and how he used to make fun of him for falling in love with a different television star each week. He felt that this must be what Robert's silly crushes felt like and that Robert would laugh at him if only he could see him now. He hadn't thought about Robert in years. It distracted him only briefly. Seren squinted at him as if she were looking at someone she was trying hard to recognize.

"Can I help you?" Seren asked calmly.

"I'm not sure." Cameron said in a surprised tone. "I mean, I'm not really sure why I…"

"Your accent!" Seren exclaimed.

Cameron was scared. He hadn't thought of disguising his voice at all and without a distinct plan other than 'find girl, grab girl, take girl home', he figured he was in deep trouble at this point. He was getting ready to turn his horse around when Seren reached out to him. "Are you from America?"

"America?" Cameron seemed stunned. He had not heard his home country mentioned in so long he had almost forgotten the sound of it. He had no idea how to respond and tried to think of something but came up short before Seren interjected.

"Do you know Robert? Are you a friend of Robert Moore?"

Cameron was now reeling. He could tell that there was no way to come up with a convincing lie at this point. His face had already revealed the answer to her question. "Y-yes. I'm a friend of Robert's."

"Do you know where he is? Is he in Gwerinatha? If he is you have to take me to him please."

The battery of questions had Cameron in shock. He could tell that Robert obviously meant something to Seren and that she desperately wanted to see him again. The thought quickly occurred to him to use this to his advantage. A lie here would make things so much easier. The idea fell into place so easily that he never once bothered thinking ahead to how he would handle the truth once the time came. He just blurted it out. "Yes. Robert is here. I can take you to him."

Seren raised both of her hands to cover her mouth. She was clearly moved to tears. "This is wonderful!" she screamed. "Just let me run and tell Samuel…"

"No!" Cam yelled while reaching down for her arm. "Robert's in trouble and we need to get back to him right away. That's why I came into town. To get help!"

Seren seemed surprised. "What kind of trouble? What does he need? Should we get a doctor?"

"Uh, no. No doctor." Cameron responded. "He uh, he just needs somebody else. Somebody from around here." Cameron was clearly at a loss but Seren was so excited at the prospect of seeing Robert again after all the passing years she willingly got on the back of Cameron's horse and rode away with him.

Cameron could not believe his luck as he sped out of town toward the farmland south of Sibridale. He not only found a beautiful girl he could consider being with but she had willingly run off with him. He tried hard to stop her from asking so many questions on the journey back. He did not want to get caught up in a lie but he knew it was just a matter of time. He kept telling her that Robert was a little further away and that it wouldn't be much longer until she would see him. He wanted to make sure she would be kept as calm as possible until they arrived at the palace. Once there he knew Jules would handle the rest as he had promised.

Chapter 23
We Need a Bigger Hero

Samuel was as pleased as he had been since news of the attacks had begun. For just a moment he could forget that Gwerinatha was at war. His mind was wrapped around seeing his most wonderful discovery, the portal key. He had found that it seemed to be in perfectly good order. He wondered aloud if there might be some use for the portal key in helping their current situation. He believed any use of the key to bring help from somewhere else could be more damaging. The cure would be far more severe than the disease since it would mean giving away the secret of their location to others. Immediately he then thought of Robert. The key had last been seen in Robert's possession. If the key was here now, where was Robert? Could Robert have returned to Gwerinatha? Was he in some sort of danger since he did not have the key? Samuel had wished he'd paid more attention to Seren when she had come into his office so long ago about the possibility of someone from Robert's world being in Gwerinatha. And what of Seren? He knew she would want to know of this immediately. He decided to try and catch her before she left for Baylies Crossing.

Samuel sent Steffan out to run the three blocks to Seren's apartment and bring her back. He knew that walking that distance at his age could take more time than he may have. An hour went by and Samuel began to worry. He thought possibly that Seren had all ready left and that Steffan had arrived too late. But even if that had been the case, Samuel reasoned, Steffan would have been back before this to let him know. He got up from his seat and looked over at the window. People were milling about less frequently now. Most of the people who had decided to leave were either packed, packing or had long since gone. It was getting dark and Samuel grew more and more nervous. Then he saw Steffan jogging down the street toward his office. Samuel ran outside to meet him.

"Steffan!" cried out Samuel, "What is that matter? Where is Seren?"

"Sh-she's gone Samuel." Steffan said trying to catch his breath.

"Here come in to the office and gather yourself. I'll fetch you a cup of tea."

"You don't understand Samuel. She's gone."

Samuel opened the door for Steffan as he made it to his seat. "What do you mean Steffan? I presume she is on her way to Baylies Crossing and you arrived too late to give her my message."

Steffan took a few deep breaths while Samuel looked at him curiously. "I wasn't too late for that Samuel." Steffan gasped.

"Here, let me get you that tea. You rest until you can speak sensibly."

Samuel returned moments later with hot tea for Steffan. He took a long sip and exhaled very slowly. "What I mean to say Samuel is that I went to her room. She hadn't left. Her things are not packed. I asked around and after some time I was able to find a witness to the fact that she left on horseback with a strange man."

"What?" exclaimed Samuel unbelievingly. "That is not like Seren! I don't..."

"There's more." Steffan interrupted. "The witness heard them talking. She didn't hear everything but she heard them mention Robert's name a time or two. She understood the man to be taking her to see Robert."

"Something is clearly amiss." replied Samuel. "If she had learned Robert was in Gwerinatha she would have come here immediately with such news.

"I would have to agree." said Steffan as he put the tea cup down on his desk. "The woman who saw them had been watching earlier from her window. She had seen the man riding around the block a few times and suspected he was up to no good. Something is definitely suspicious about all this."

"Yes. I must get in touch with Urien at once."

"Just exactly what I was thinking." said Urien as he walked into Samuel's office from the street.

"Urien, my boy!" exclaimed Samuel. "I am more than happy to see you now. We have just learned of some upsetting news about Seren that involves a stranger."

"My cousin?" replied Urien. "Where is she? What has happened?"

"She has been taken by a stranger, possibly from America."

"No!" screamed Urien. "This cannot be! Dear Samuel I came to see you to give you news that we had gotten concerning the enemy and now I fear it to be all the worse!"

"Whatever do you mean son?"

"We gathered intelligence from some of our soldiers imbued with the light of the blue orb. They have learned of a camp in the farmlands to the southwest of Sibridale. In that camp were many creatures from the Unfinished Lands. Before they departed back to

the south we were able to learn from them of a man named
Cameron who came from another world. This man is leading them
in an all-out attack on Gwerinatha. They mean to eradicate each
and every one us Samuel. This isn't about anything other than
complete annihilation of humankind. Cameron is their general and
has a battle lust unlike any I have ever encountered. If my cousin is
with him she is in grave danger indeed." Samuel slumped into his
chair and began to turn white.

"What have I done?" Samuel moaned quietly. "Poor Seren. What
is to become of her?"

Urien knelt down on one knee and looked in Samuel's
downturned face. "This is not a time to be weak sir. Seren is my
cousin and I could not be angrier or more frustrated at this turn of
events but this is a time for action. That is why I came to see you.
To give you this news and to ask, no, demand a favor."

"What could that possibly be Urien?" Samuel said barely
composed.

"It is has been said that anyone bathed in the light of all three
orbs simultaneously is given the powers of all three permanently. If
this is true I dare to be bathed thusly so as to combat Cameron
directly. It is our only chance!"

"What you ask for is dangerous Urien." Samuel whispered. "We
do not know for sure if this will even work, the orbs are not as
powerful as they once were."

"I cannot believe that danger is even a question at this point
Samuel. "With all due respect, how much danger can there be past
complete human eradication? I don't believe we have many options
and I am more than willing to take on the chance."

Samuel stayed quiet. Once again he knew there was
unfortunately no other choice but to risk Urien's life on a chance the
three orbs could give him the power to defeat Cameron and turn
back his armies. He wanted there to be another way. He wanted
badly for some other idea to come into his wise old head but none
would come. Slowly he stood up and putting his hands around
Urien's neck he agreed to help in anyway he could.

Samuel was the only one who fully understood the inner
workings of the orbs since he was the one the Originators had given
them to in the first place. It was Samuel who taught the soldiers
how long to be in the light and where to stand, etc. for the best
possible results. He had Steffan and Urien gather the orbs in the
same room and he situated them so as to give the permanent light
effect to Urien. He had Urien stand in the middle of the room and
he and Steffan opened the plates on the spheres to allow the orbs'
light to shine directly on Urien.

At first, Urien felt nothing. The light shone white around his midsection where the red, blue and green lights converged. He seemed to be tickled at first and then mildly irritated. He fidgeted a bit as if he had been in a sleeping bag with itching powder for a while. Then he began to tremble as if he were having a great cold chill. All at once he let out a shriek and slumped to the floor. Steffan and Samuel immediately shut off the orbs' light and attended to him.

He lay unconscious for three minutes and when he awoke he jumped to his feet.

"How do you feel Urien?" inquired Samuel.

Urien looked around the room and then flexed his muscles, stretched his back and grinned. "I have never felt better Samuel. I feel power surging throughout me. I feel as if I could take on an entire army by myself."

"Well that seems to be the desired intent." Steffan remarked. Samuel gave Steffan a disapproving look and took a few steps back from Urien.

"Now Urien... what am I thinking?" asked Samuel. "Concentrate."

Urien closed his eyes tightly and began to concentrate. "You are worried. You are thinking that the orbs' waning power may have some unknown side effects. Samuel, don't worry. I have the power now. I only need it long enough to take care of the army and then whatever happens to me is fine. I can deal with that if I know Gwerinatha is safe."

"Very well Urien. We can see the intuitive power is working. Now think about my desk. Concentrate on it and lift it off the ground."

"Yes", said Urien. "I feel like I can do just that." Urien focused his mind on the desk and it slowly began to rise first one and then two feet off the ground.

"Excellent." Samuel said. I think you may be all right after all. But promise me you will work on your abilities and learn your limitations before you engage in battle."

"I will not have much time I'm afraid." Urien responded. "But I will do what I can on the way to the farmlands. I must get going as soon as possible if there is to be any hope of saving Seren."

Urien quickly left Samuel to gather as many men as possible to take off after Cameron and Seren. Samuel looked out the window at the setting sun and hung his head. He then went back over to the orbs and noticed their light fading.

Chapter 24
You Won't Get Away With This

Seren began to get a little nervous. While riding on the back of Cameron's horse for what seemed like hours she had asked many unanswered questions. She was beginning to think something wasn't quite right. "Can you at least tell me your name?" she asked hoping this simple question would get a reply. "I mean all I know is that you are a friend of Robert's."

"Yeah, me and Robert go way back." Cameron paused before continuing. He didn't want to show his nervousness. "The name's Cameron Gray."

"How did you get here Cameron? And when did Robert return?"

"Look, I know you're curious and you've asked me that last question at least a half dozen times. Don't worry about it. That's all."

By this point Seren was *really* getting nervous. She realized something was not right with the situation and was wishing she had stuck to her initial feelings and had gone to see Samuel with the news of Robert's return. At least then she would have someone she trusted along. Now she was beginning to feel all alone. Then she caught a glimpse of the farmland. She hadn't had too much experience with farms before and her travels had led her past them but not through them. Still she thought something looked out of place on this farm. She saw in the distance odd large shapes lying all around. As they got closer she could feel Cameron tensing up and she began to worry. She could now see what looked like large cocoons all over the farm where crops would normally be growing. Even more disturbing to her were the grayish men with no faces tending the cocoons.

"What is all this?" she asked, her voice showing signs of fear.

"Listen, it's better if you just don't worry, like I told you." Cameron said tersely.

Seren started to squirm and tried to jump off the horse before Cameron could make a complete stop. Two temp men rushed to the scene and grabbed her before she could get to the ground. Seren screamed but got no reaction from the faceless soulless temp men. Cameron, still on horse back, yelled out orders to them. "Put her in the barn while I inspect the cocoons."

The temp men took Seren into a large red wooden barn. She fought them as best she could but they each one were too strong for her and the two of them easily took her without much trouble. Cameron could hear her screaming the whole way into the barn but he seemed not to notice. The closer he got to the cocoons the more intense his focus became.

Cameron looked pleased at the work the temp men were doing. In order to build an army large enough to attack a city the size of New London the portable machines that built the cocoons were not enough. Now the temp men themselves were duplicating the machinery and creating ten times as many cocoons which they had spread all across the farm. Cameron took several minutes to walk around and look over them. He didn't have the time or intention of checking every single one but he would stop at every third row or so and look the cocoons over carefully. He nodded a bit at each stop and gave thumbs up to each of the temp men whose work he would stop long enough to be checked. Once he was fully satisfied he walked back to the barn. He stopped before going inside and took a long look over the entire farm now covered in cocoons. He took in a deep breath and let it out slowly. He had never felt more certain of himself. The excitement of the battle to come overwhelmed him for a moment and he grinned widely. Then he turned and slowly walked into the barn and his confidence abruptly vanished.

Immediately Seren began screaming at him from her makeshift jail cell made out of a stable. "Hey! Let me out of here! What are you doing!?! What do you want with me? Answer me! I demand that you answer me at once!"

She had two temp men guarding the locked gate. They stood motionless with their hands down by their sides completely ignoring her remarks.

"Listen, I know this looks bad..." Cameron began.

"Looks bad!?!" Seren screamed. "Looks bad!?! You lied to me to get me to come with you and you throw me in a stable and lock me inside with two, two, whatever those things are..."

"I know." Cameron said with his hand motioning her to calm down. "Like I said it looks bad. But really, you'll see this isn't as bad as it seems."

"You're barmy!" Seren shouted. "I don't even want to know what all those things are out on the farm but you're clearly insane! And what have you done with Robert? Where is he? I want to see him!"

"Please. Just try to be calm. I'm sorry I lied to you. I promise that's the last time. I won't need to lie to you ever again. I just had to get you to come with me that's all."

"Do you even know Robert?"

"Yes, of course. That wasn't a lie. But I don't know where he is. Honest I don't ."

Seren crossed her arms and looked at Cameron gruffly. She stared a hole into his face and didn't blink for what seemed like several minutes.

"Really. My friend Robert came here many years ago with a portal key that was handed down in his family. He opened up a dimensional doorway and walked right through it. He was only gone for a couple of seconds and then he came right back. I thought I'd try it since he didn't seem to have been gone long at all. I grabbed the portal key from him and came through myself. I've since lost the key and been here for I don't even know how many years. And that's the truth. Honest."

Seren had looked away from him but still had her arms crossed. Her eyebrows furrowed and she had a look of disgust on her face. She looked down at the ground and then slowly looked back at Cameron.

"I'm beginning to think that Robert was here for more than just a few seconds." Cameron said sheepishly. "I have thought about it over the years and even though it didn't dawn on me when I ran into this fool place he did seem to look different. It was like his clothes had shifted on him a little or something. I can't really put my finger on it but he definitely looked a little different." Seren said nothing. "So I guess if you knew him then I must have been right. He must have been here a while, is that right?"

"If you think I'm going to answer any of your questions you are crazier than I first anticipated." Seren replied. "I will tell you that I believe your story for now." She looked off into the stable again. "There's enough of it that rings true. But you'll get nothing from me."

"That's where you're wrong." Cameron muttered under his breath.

"What's that ?" Seren asked.

"Never mind. It's almost nightfall and you'll want to get some rest. This is where you'll be bedding down I'm afraid."

"What? How am I supposed to sleep now, after all this? You're having me on, right?"

"Suit yourself." Cameron said. "I'm going to bed down on this hay over in the corner. If you sleep, you sleep, if not, oh well."

Cameron walked over to the corner of the barn and began preparing a bed in the hay. Two more fresh temp men came in and took the place of the two that were guarding Seren who were beginning to get a little mottled. Seren did not notice in the dusk. With a fresh batch of temp men growing just outside Cameron had no worries about them running down on him. He could sleep easily, or so he thought.

Chapter 25
The Battles Wax and Wane and Wax Again

In the morning Cameron was awakened with a battle cry. He heard the clang of swords and axes along with a few stray gunshots. One of the Unfinished Land creatures came into the barn to give Cameron the news. "The humans have come general! They are battling the temporary men as we speak."

Cameron quickly got into his armor while the creature continued. "I brought my men back at the appointed time as you requested to prepare for the next battle."

"Are they all here?"

"Yes sir, well mostly. I have ten score of my fellows at the waiting. Three score are with me now and the rest are on their way."

"Good." Cameron said as he finished fastening his breastplate. "I need you to take this woman back to the palace. Take her to Jules and make sure she isn't harmed."

"No!" screamed Seren in the background. She hadn't slept a wink all night and the sounds of gunshots though disturbing at first gave her hope that she may be rescued.

Cameron ordered three very large and frightening looking
creatures to escort Seren to Jules' palace. She kicked and screamed
as they yanked her from the stable. The largest creature that
appeared to be stronger than the rest casually picked Seren up and
threw her over his shoulder. She began yelling and slamming her
fists on the creature's back. However his hide was thick and tough
and she only ended up hurting her fists. Eventually she stopped but
kept screaming until she could scream no more.

Cameron grabbed his sword and shield and stormed out of the
barn. He could see fighting in the distance. "So! They're bringing the
battle to us! All right! I'm more than ready for this fight. Bring it
on!" He called for his horse, quickly mounted it and began riding off
toward the combatants. He could see a lot of temp men falling left
and right. The enemy had learned how to take them out and had
sharpshooters going straight for their heads. Even with such an
advantage the temp men still far outnumbered the guard. Cameron
could see the humans were strong and were capable of taking on
more than one temp man at a time. He called for the creatures of
the Unfinished Lands to fan out and attack the humans from the
sides while he and the temp men occupied them up the middle.

Cameron noticed there were some temp men that seemed to be
floating in the air. He thought he saw many of them flying up into
the air of their own accord. He couldn't spend time worrying with it
as he had gotten to the point where he was meeting some of the
enemy head on. He rode hard directly toward one of the men on
horseback who was shooting directly at him. The bullets that did
manage to find their way toward Cameron bounced off his armor.
He kept riding directly at his assailant until he was close enough to
slash at him with his sword. The man's gun went flying through the
air and Cam immediately spun his horse around and rode back
toward him. Cam almost fell off the horse due to his inexperience at
riding the Gwerinathan version. After regaining control he charged
at the shooter now bleeding profusely from his hand and stabbed
him in the chest.

Cameron seemed to enjoy the thrill of this battle even more
than the rest. Minute after minute, victory after victory he savored
every moment. He never seemed to tire at all. The guard were doing
their best to take out a lot of the temp men but for every one they
shot down there seemed to them to be two more to take their place.
The cocoons were opening as fast as they could and each temp man
that burst forth from them was instantly ready for battle. Soon the
guard had run out of ammo and had to begin fighting hand to hand.
Here they had a slight edge in the battle due to the powers
bestowed on them from the orbs. With so many temp men coming at
such a pace the battle lasted longer than the guard had anticipated

and soon many of them were running out of power. They had put a fairly large dent in the amount of temp men by the time the creatures of the Unfinished Lands had engaged them from the sides.

The battle took another turn as the guard found themselves battling creatures from one side and temp men from another. The creatures did not break so easily as the temp men but neither were they as quick or agile. The guard had done a good job until now at keeping even with the enemy but soon their numbers started dwindling.

Cameron looked around with a smile as the creatures moved in to aid the temp men. He felt like it would only be a matter of moments before they would conquer the guard completely. Then he noticed something on the horizon: even more humans coming to engage in the battle. He saw farmers and workers with tools and even what he thought to be some women and children. For a brief moment he felt a twinge of sympathy and then quickly disregarded it. He still felt that even though they may help in conquering the creatures that the vast amount of temp men now being manufactured would turn the tide in the end. He felt this was only a prolonging of the inevitable. To be certain though he sent a few of the temp men back to get word to the others who had taken Seren away. He wanted every available creature that could fight to be at this battle.

Then he saw temp men flying around again. He had thought it was just his eyes playing tricks earlier but now he had seen it again. And this time it was getting closer. Cameron turned his attention away from the guardsman he had just slain to see just what was causing this occurrence. The closer it got the more confused he got until he saw Urien seemingly throwing temp men around without touching them. Once the general's eyes made contact with Cameron he began to charge straight for him.

"Well, now." Cameron said with a smirk. "This just went from fantastic to totally awesome!"

He charged at Urien who was already coming full bore at him. Urien then raised his hands out and Cameron noticed his horse's feet go out from under him. Immediately the horse fell over and it was all Cameron could do to roll away to keep from being crushed by the muscular steed. "Oh, you wanna play rough do ya?" Cameron ran at the feet of Urien's horse and slashed at its front legs. The horse reared up and Urien fell backwards. Somehow Urien managed to land on his feet and came running at Cameron which startled him long enough to be put on his heels. The two began a vicious swordfight with neither seeming to gain any ground.

"Where is my cousin you fiend? What have you done with her?"

Urien screamed at Cameron during a moment when he had him down on the ground. Cameron flipped himself upright and put Urien in a similar situation.

"I don't know what you're talking about!"

"Seren. The girl you took from New London!" Urien retorted as he kicked Cameron off of him. "She is my cousin and I mean to bring her home safely!"

"Well she's not here right now." Cam then went after Urien with a lunge. Urien leapt out of the way.

"Where is she then? Tell me quickly and your suffering shall be at a minimum."

"The only guy doing any suffering around here is going to be you!" Cam yelled as he flew back at Urien swords clanging.

Urien had tried several times during the battle to lift Cameron into the air but found that it was impossible. He had also tried to read Cameron's thoughts but found that too wasn't working. He reached out and threw several temp men away from him while fighting Cameron and thus realized that his power had not waned but instead some force was keeping the power from having any effect on Cameron.

"What's wrong buddy?" Cameron asked him. "Are you getting tired? Are your mama's boy girlie legs turning to jelly on you?"

"I've heard your insolent manner of speech before!" Urien shouted as he attacked Cameron again.

"Geez! Robert must have really gotten around while he was here!"

"Robert! Of course! You are from his world. America is it not?" Urien asked while mentally throwing two temp men at Cameron's feet.

Cam tripped and fell over the temp men and looked up at Urien moving in for another attack. He quickly spun around and defended the potential death blow with his shield. "Yeah, that's right! America! A place you dirty sub humans will never live to see once my men and I get finished here."

The individual fight between Cam and Urien gradually moved away from the rest of the battles. Urien intentionally kept moving Cameron back further away from the cocoons for fear he had some sort of mental power over the temp men. They were already backed up behind the barn before Cameron realized what was happening. Then they both heard screaming in the distance. It was Seren. She had wrestled free from the temp men who had replaced the creatures who had taken her. Those creatures were now moving toward the battle behind Urien and Cameron. In the heat of the moment Cam didn't realize that the temp men he had sent after Seren were two that were nearing the end of their life cycle. Once they got weak enough she was able to overpower them.

"Urien!" screamed Seren running toward them.

"Stay back cousin!" Urien shouted. "This man is very dangerous. He is the leader of our attackers."

"Well you got that right." Cam retorted. "I am more dangerous than you know!"

Cam got his head down and shoved into Urien's midsection like a battering ram. Once he was on the ground Cam got up and ran toward Seren who was getting closer but stopped in her tracks. He then grabbed her arm and twisted it behind her and spun her around in front of him. He then began to walk backwards with her.

"Now listen here cousin." Cam shouted back. "I am taking this girl with me and nobody is stopping me." Seren screamed but he just kept walking backwards dragging her feet which were kicking up dust. In the meantime a dozen temp men had made their way from the barn to Urien and attacked him before he could get up. "Nothing like a good dog pile." Cam said as he yanked Seren along with him.

"Like I said before, you just need to trust me. One day you'll look back on all this and laugh. I promise you."

Chapter 26
The Showdown

While Urien struggled to get out from under the temp men Cameron had two others assist him with Seren. They used some rope from the barn to bind her hands and the two of them then carried her behind Cameron and they headed back toward the Unfinished Lands.

Urien had begun to lift several of the temp men off of himself with his orb abilities but several more pounced on him in their place. It took him several minutes to get them all subdued and then he looked around but saw no sign of Cameron or Seren. He looked back at the battle and saw his men were in desperate need. He looked back in the direction he had last seen Cameron. He knew then what he had to do. "Damn!" he shouted as he kicked the ground. He shook his sword in the air. "This is not over foul one! You and yours will be dealt with soon enough!" The words did not soothe him any as he then ran back to aide his men as their numbers were beginning to dwindle against the enemy.

"Hold tight men! We have only to hold them until reinforcements arrive! Aim for their heads! Aim for their heads!"

***

After a few hours of traveling Cameron stopped to rest. They had finally made their way across the river and into the Unfinished Lands. He had the temp men watch over Seren while he went out hunting for food. She sat under a tree her hands bound and stared intently at the temp men. It did her no good to try and get a reaction from them as they had no faces and no souls. She soon realized they were little more than machines despite their organic state.

Cameron came back not long after he left with a couple of rabbits to cook on a fire he had made. As he worked on getting a fire started he could sense Seren staring at him. He ignored her as best he could. After the meat was skinned and cooked he offered some to her and she flatly refused.

While he ate he thought he'd return the favor and stare back at Seren. Only he didn't give her the same menacing look she had given him. After a few minutes of this unbalanced staring contest Seren had had enough. "Stop looking at me like that!" she exclaimed. "You are unnerving me."

"Sorry lady." Cameron said. "You know you're kind of cute when you get angry."

"Augh!" screamed Seren. "I can't stand this any longer! You have to let me go! I must return home at once!"

"Oh you're goin' home sweetie. It's just a new home. You'll get to like it after a while."

Seren's stare changed immediately. Her mouth dropped a bit as she realized just what Cameron was intending. "You don't mean I am going to live with you?"

"Oh it's better than you think. I live in a beautiful palace in the Unfinished Lands. We'll have lots of servants. Ugly as sin, but hey they work for cheap."

"The Unfinished Lands?" Seren screamed. "It's worse than I thought."

"We don't have to stay there. We've got all the land we could ever want. I may even expand and start rebuilding this whole place. We can build a newer more beautiful palace anywhere you like."

"I would not live with you if you were the last man in all of Gwerinatha."

"You know it's funny." Cameron said as he leaned back to pick food from his teeth with a small twig. "I have heard people say things like that a lot. But the truth is you just never know what you'd do in a situation like that until it comes to pass. You, my lucky lady, are going to get such a chance. You see, in a matter of weeks I *will* be the last man in Gwerinatha."

***

Hour after hour the brave men of Gwerinatha battled against the creatures and temp men. Soon only a few left were battling with any orb abilities. The rest were beginning to struggle. All the advantage they had gained had since been lost with the arrival of the creature army. Urien fought bravely however and gave the men great hope. He had those who still had abilities to follow him to the source of the temp men. The others he instructed to stay behind and battle the much slower creatures.

While he was ripping through several temp men at a time he could hear cheers in the background. Samuel and Gefell had appeared with more soldiers. It was clear that some of these had fresh orb abilities and some even had guns with more ammunition.

The cavalry had arrived. Urien worked his way from the battle back toward the reinforcements.

"Samuel!" Urien called out. "Is this it? Is this the last of our men?"

"I'm afraid so Urien. Other than those hiding out in the mountains who could not be reached this amounts to the total sum of our available fighting men of Gwerinatha."

Urien scoured the men and realized despite the positive effect on morale their appearance made, their numbers might be enough to win this battle but perhaps not the war. He then looked at Samuel staring down at the ground for a second. "Is there something else Samuel? What is it?"

"It is the orbs Urien. They have lost all their power. I had been afraid of using them all at once for the power they might use up as well as what side effects might be endowed to the subject. And after you left I saw the light fading. I got as many people as I could to bathe in what was left of their light. Then the light from all the orbs went dim completely."

Urien looked down at the ground himself. Then he raised his head and looked rather stern. "It will have to do. I'm going to go after Cameron."

"Are you sure that's wise son?"

"This isn't just about rescuing Seren. He is the head of this snake and it has to be cut off if we are to win this war! I'll get a few of the men you brought to come with me. I have discovered that there are cocoons and machinery that creates these temp men. I have destroyed as many as I could. I need as many as possible to go after the rest."

***

Cameron put out the fire and began to clean away as much evidence from the ground as possible. He seemed perturbed that Seren didn't eat anything. "You're going to need your strength you know. It's a long walk back to the palace." Seren did not respond. "The Unfinished Lands are very dangerous of course, what with all the weird creatures and plants and moving rocks and trees and everything. But you know the closer to the palace we get, the more insane it gets." Seren looked away in silence. "Don't be frightened of the Unfinished Lands. As long as you're with me you'll be safe."

"I'm hardly frightened of them. Robert and I survived the Unfinished Lands years ago!" Seren snapped.

"Ah! So you are speaking to me." Cameron said with a smirk.

"I'd do more than speak if I had my hands free."

"Yeah, I bet you would." Cameron stared at her silently for a moment. "You'd probably try to kill me if I wasn't careful. But that won't be a concern for long. Jules will take all the fight out of you. You'll be made into the perfect little wife."

Seren spat at Cameron and it landed at his feet. He stared down at it and then looked up to the sky as if he was remembering something. "You know, I think I saw a movie like that once. Yeah, I remember it now. All the perfect little wives in this town. That's just what Jules is going to turn you into for me. It makes sense now."

"I'll never be your wife! I'd sooner die than give you such a privilege."

"My, my. We are getting uppity now aren't we?" Cameron had the temp men pick Seren up from where she was seated next to a large tree. While they were holding her he leaned in and grabbed her chin with his hand. He then stared deep into her eyes as she scowled. "I just wanted to see that fire within you one last time before it goes out. No. I won't miss it." She pulled her face away in disgust as he turned to leave. "C'mon guys. The sooner we get going the sooner we get back and I can begin making my wedding plans. No wait, that's a girl thing. You can do that after you get reformed. Yeah, you'd probably like that then."

Then a noise like a branch breaking and leaves rustling startled Cameron. "What's that?" Cam said as he wheeled around. He saw nothing and then looked back at the two temp men who were holding Seren. One after the other each of them stiffened up and fell over. Seren shrieked. Cameron turned around quickly to see Urien and two of his men each with smoking guns held tightly in their hands.

"So! You've made it back from the battle I see." Cameron said slyly.

"Come behind us Seren." Urien said calmly motioning to his men. Seren obliged and one of the men untied her bonds.

"You know those pop guns won't work on me in this armor." Cameron said with confidence.

Urien said nothing but stared blankly at Cameron. Cam began walking slowly around with his sword held out high and his knees bent. "Now c'mon buddy. You think three against one is fair?"

Urien looked back at Seren who was rubbing her wrist just above a clenched fist. "I'd say that's four against one and doubt you have the slightest clue as to what is or is not fair."

"You may be right about that." Cam said as he reached down to the pick up some ashes from the fire he'd just put out and blew them at Urien's face. The other two men now reloaded, both shot Cameron but the bullets bounced off his armor. He ran toward them and knocked Urien's legs out from under him while he was still blinded from the ashes. He then rapidly swung his sword around and slashed at one of the two guards. The second guard rushed him but he kicked him back out of the way and he fell over Urien who had just begun to get to his feet. He then stabbed the first guard in the heart and quickly turned his attention to Urien and the second guard who were both now on the ground.

"Oh, come on now." Cameron said. "Don't make this too easy for me. After all this looks like the big game changing moment. You don't want to disappoint me now, especially in front of our audience." Cam motioned toward Seren who had crouched down behind the body of the slain guard weeping.

Urien then got to his feet and rushed toward Cam who easily dodged out of the way. Cam then dodged the second guard who had followed suit. He then spun around to face them both. As they walked closer to him they slowed down and began to move to either side. When they got close enough Cam leapt into the air and kicked out both legs hitting each of his opponents and knocking them to the ground. He then stabbed the second guard in the heart eliciting another shriek from Seren and then felt a sharp pain on his back. Urien had brought his sword down hard against Cameron but his armor protected him from any damage. He faced Urien and they began to lock swords.

Urien had tried again to use his abilities on Cameron but to no avail. He realized the armor had to be the cause of it and tried to knock Cam's helmet off with his sword. "Ah, straight for the head. You ain't messin' around are you?" Cam yelled at him. "You know I've found most of the guys on this world to be fairly wimpy with their fighting styles. None of them would last two days out here. But you're different. You have what it takes." Cam ducked down as Urien swung his sword over his head again. He then quickly sprang up and kicked Urien back several feet.

"I find your fighting style to be that of a coward." Urien said as he quickly got back to his feet. Urien saw a vine next to Seren that seemed to be moving. "Seren look out!" She jumped out of the way recognizing the cornleash vine and knowing what it meant to do to her. She grabbed a knife from one of the dead guard and cut the vine before it could grab her feet.

Cameron turned to watch Seren. "Yeah, some tricky things out here. You need to be careful."

Urien then got the idea to use his abilities to get the vines to come around Cameron as he slowly walked towards him. He managed to get the vines to get close to Cameron's feet but then they stopped. Urien looked down in amazement as the vines were seemingly no longer under his control. Cameron saw Urien's puzzled look and then looked at his feet. "Oh, you were trying to get them to help you?" Cam asked rhetorically. "That's not gonna work. You see, all these bizarre plants and creatures in the Unfinished Lands... they're friends of mine. They'd never hurt me. But you..., well now that's another story."

Just then a tree that had been several feet behind Urien began rapidly moving toward him. It pushed Urien as he looked behind him in surprise. As it rapidly pushed him toward Cameron he held his sword out and easily ran it through Urien's midsection. The tree then went back to where it was just as rapidly as it had come forth. Urien slumped to the ground and Cameron took his sword with two hands, fell to his knees and shoved it into Urien's back.

"A guy like this, you want to make sure the job is done right." Cameron said as he got to his feet. He then began walking toward Seren who was now in hysterics.

"Calm down sweetie. We're just gonna take a breather here and then you and I will be off once again. I promise you this will all be like a pleasant memory some day if you even remember it at all."

Chapter 27
Escape a Fate Worse Than Death

Seren took off running north. She knew she wouldn't stand a chance fighting Cameron and her only hope was to get away while he was recovering from the battle. He gave chase but he still hadn't fully caught his breath from fighting Urien. Seren was able to get a significant lead on him. She ran as hard as she could for several minutes and then began to tire. She collapsed behind a large tree and hoped for a second wind. She looked behind her to see any sign of Cameron but there was none. She knew he would not give up so easily and began to struggle to get back to her feet. Just then she heard the sound of people running. At first she wasn't quite sure which direction it was coming from. It wasn't long before she realized that it was coming from in front of her. Her first instinct was to hide behind the tree but she was too frightened that Cameron may see her if she did. She squinted hard to see if she could make out any figures in the distance.

"Seren!" a voice called out.

"Seren?" another voice echoed.

She instantly recognized the voices of Samuel and Gefell. She didn't answer back for fear that Cameron was close enough to hear her. Instead she ran toward the voices while looking back to see if she was being followed. Two of the guards who were escorting Samuel and Gefell ran in front of them and grabbed Seren and pulled her behind them.

Seren began crying in Samuel's arms.

"You're safe now dear. Worry not."

She began crying even harder.

"Maybe she won't feel safe until we've gotten out of the Unfinished Lands." Gefell's left mouth spoke out.

"I know I won't feel safe until we're back in New London." his right mouth added.

"No, no." Samuel said quietly. "There is something else. Where is Urien lass? Why is he not here with you?"

She began crying even louder and harder at the mention of her cousin's name.

And then a voice answered from the distance. "Urien cannot protect her now old man. And I doubt seriously you will be able to either."

"Killer!" Seren shouted as she ripped free from Samuel's embrace. "He killed Urien and the others! He's the one responsible for all the attacks!"

At once the two guards who were in front ran to attack Cameron. Two more guards who were escorting from the rear joined after. Samuel ran after Seren for fear she too would try to fight.

"Come girl. We had best hide away somewhere."

"Run and hide?" Seren questioned. "But Urien!"

"We can do nothing for him dear. And if we want to survive we will have to make haste."

He grabbed Seren by the arm and took her and Gefell away from the battle. Cameron was tired from all the previous battles and after the chase of Seren, but the guards had a new surge of adrenaline. The battle wouldn't take terribly long but it would be long enough to find a place to hide away. They found a cave that seemed stable enough. It wasn't as posh as the one that Samuel had decorated to be a home but it didn't have any other creatures living in it at the time.

Gefell looked around finding the place to be a bit cramped. "Any port in a storm I guess." his right mouth said.

"I tell you I don't like this place." his left mouth added.

"It will have to do Gefell." Samuel said. "Now be quiet. We must listen for the others."

They all stayed quiet for several minutes and heard nothing. Seren looked as if she were about to speak but then Samuel cautioned her with a finger to his lips. They looked around for a moment, eyes darting back and forth nervously in the dark dank cave. Nothing seemed to be happening. Had Cameron defeated the other guards they wondered? Had they thrown Cameron off? They couldn't be sure and the silence began to get to them. Just before either of Gefell's mouths could take no more of the quiet and burst into words a distinct rumbling sound started from the cave floor. Seren and Samuel's eyes widened as the floor started to vibrate. She began to worry about a reappearance of the worms from an earlier cave experience. But this was different. No worms came up from the cave floor. Instead the cave floor began to shift and widen. It slowly dropped several feet and turned slightly so that their view of the cave entrance was blocked. And then everything stopped.

With her arms against the cave wall and knees bent Seren slowly looked around without moving. She didn't want to so much as exhale until she could be sure nothing would move again. Samuel similarly was motionless and silent. Gefell could not brace himself against the wall as the humans had done. He was jostled during the ordeal and found himself less fearful of making sound at this point.

"What was that all about?" his right mouth inquired.

"I think our cave has just resituated itself." his left mouth added. "Dang fool Unfinished Lands!"

Samuel shushed him and reminded him that Cameron was still out there.

"I don't think he can hear us now." Gefell's left mouth responded. We're too far down and the cave door is practically closed."

"Instead I should think our worry would be how we are going to get out of here!" Gefell's left mouth pointed out.

Samuel took a few steps out to make sure the ground was solid and no longer moving. He then felt around until he came across Gefell's pack.

"Hey watch it!"

"I'm just reaching for a lantern Gefell." Samuel told him. "There is no need for undue excitement."

"We're stuck in a cave that just lowered us further in the ground, we can't see the opening, there's a mad warrior looking to kill us and you say there is no reason for undue excitement!" Gefell's right mouth retorted.

"I would have to ask what measure of due excitement you may allow us?" his left mouth added.

Samuel grabbed the lantern from the pack and lit it. He held it up to see a surprising hint of a grin on Seren's face.

"I had forgotten how amusing your prattle could be friend Gefell." Seren said as she stroked his feathered mane. She leaned her head against his. "Don't worry Gefell. Things have a way of working out for the best."

"That's easy for you to say." Gefell's left mouth replied. "You have the ability to climb."

"I am not so certain there will be a need for any of us to climb Gefell." Samuel said with an authoritative tone. "You will recall I have had a rather lengthy experience with the phenomena of the Unfinished Lands and I am no longer worried about the predicament we find ourselves in at the bottom of this cave. Actually I find it quite serendipitous if you'll pardon the pun."

"Whatever do you mean Samuel?" Seren asked.

"Well the timing of the whole event. It seemed to save us from the wrath of the leader of these genocidal attacks. It took a while for it to sink in."

Seren and Gefell looked at each other with confusion and then back at Samuel who was taking his time carefully examining the cave walls. "Sorry, that pun was unintentional as well. You see it has been many years since my self imposed exile to the Unfinished Lands and I had almost forgotten that there are sometimes patterns to the way in which the flora and fauna misbehave as it were."

"Could you be a little less cryptic and a little more assuring?" Gefell's right mouth inquired.

"Yes, yes of course." Samuel went on. "This new position of the cave is only temporary. I have no idea how long it shall be this way but it will in fact change back to the way that it was. Or at least close enough that we will be able to crawl out the way we crawled in. Now keep in mind we may have another shift or two in which we go deeper into the ground but I am absolutely certain that it is only for a short time."

"But perhaps long enough for the killer to have gone on his way." Gefell's left mouth replied.

"No." Seren said nervously. "He won't give up. At least not for long. We may be down here long enough for him to go back to his palace or somewhere but eventually he'll come looking for me again."

"What was that, you said about a palace dear?"

"He said he had some kind of palace he was taking me to live in. He said someone there named Jules was going to fix me so that I would be some sort of obedient spouse or something. Can you imagine the horror Samuel? Samuel?"

Samuel slumped to the ground of the cave unblinking.

"Samuel?" Gefell's left and right mouths added one after the other.

He sat quietly for a minute and still without blinking he uttered something the others could barely hear. "He is back. Gule is back. I cannot believe it."

Chapter 29
The End is Near

Still slumped in the corner of the cave, Samuel's eyes glazed over as Gefell and Seren tried to make sense of it all.

"What's wrong with him Seren?" Gefell's right mouth asked.

"It's as if he doesn't even know we're here." his left mouth added.

"Who is it?" Seren asked Samuel. "Who is back? Tell us what's going on."

Samuel blinked for the first time in minutes and then put his head into his hand. He nodded left and right and then slowly looked back up at the others. "I am sorry my friends. I had not meant to add more worry upon you with the hour already so dark."

Seren knelt down beside Samuel and put her hand on his shoulder. "What did I say Samuel? What is it about the palace that upset you so?"

"Palace?" Samuel questioned as if he hadn't even heard her utter the word. "I do not know how to answer young one. So much has changed now. So much is the matter."

"Can't you tell us anything?" Gefell's left mouth wondered.

"Give it to us straight Samuel. We can take it. What could

possibly be worse than the situation we find ourselves in now?" Gefell's right mouth added.

Samuel took in a large breath and let out a long sigh. "I wish that it was an easy thing to tell you dear ones. But in reality this day seems far worse than I had originally thought. You see the Originators were not all friendly to humans. They did not all look kindly on us being here. One in particular as I recall was quite adamant that we ruined everything they had planned and wanted very much to rid Gwerinatha of our presence." Samuel's voice trailed off as his gaze fell to the floor. "I fear he is finally doing just that."

"What do you mean Samuel?" asked Seren. "Cameron is the leader of the attacks on Gwerinatha. He is human and came from Robert's world.

"Robert's world." echoed Samuel. "That's it. You will be safe this day my daughter in spirit."

"What on earth are you going on about Samuel? We've got to get out of this cave and find Cameron and stop him before he destroys our world."

Samuel got to his feet and turned away from the others and thought silently for a while. Seren got up and put her arm around Gefell.

"I don't like this Gefell. He's not answering my questions."

"You think senility has finally set in after so many centuries?" Gefell's right mouth asked.

"You would have thought it might have started up at least a couple hundred years before now." his left mouth chimed in.

"Now, now, Gefell." Seren said as she patted his head. "I appreciate any attempts to ease the tension at the moment but this is far too serious. More is wrong than we know and Samuel holds the key."

"The key." Samuel muttered. "Yes, the key." He patted a pouch he had on his side. He then turned to Seren and put his arms squarely on her shoulders. "My dear Seren, I want you to be safe above all else and you will be."

"Samuel, you aren't making any sense to me."

"You mentioned a Jules, Seren. He was meant to change you into a wife for Cameron. I am afraid as bad as that would be if it happened at all you would be killed soon after."

"What?!?"

"Listen to me." Samuel said as his hands slid down her shoulders and gripped her forearms tightly. "Jules is a rogue Originator. His actual name is Gule. He never wanted there to be humans in Gwerinatha. He has great power and he is the one responsible for the genocide of our people. Cameron is but a pawn in his plan and all of the creatures of the Unfinished Lands will do his bidding. I am certain that after Cameron and his armies destroy the last of the humans Cameron too will be killed. Gule hates us and would not even want to see one human living in this place."

Seren grew even more terrified than she had been in the last two days. She had never seen the look in Samuel's eyes that stared back at her made all the more frightful with the lantern light coming from below. She wondered if he was capable of rational thought. She blinked a few times and shrugged her shoulders until Samuel loosened his grip. He picked up the lantern and swung it around looking up at the top of the cave. The lantern next to his face made a fearful moment all the more chilling.

"I do not know how much time we have left my child."

"Oh, please Samuel. You're scaring me. Stop talking like that."

"I fear the situation is too grave. I must tell you only what you need to know." He reached into his pouch and pulled out the portal key.

"You have the key!" Seren said as her heart pounded with newfound excitement. "We can go for help."

"No dear. You do not understand. There is no help for Gwerinatha. Our people are doomed. We do not have the forces left to stand up against the armies of Gule. Even if there were time to gather all the men who hide in the mountains and all the men who live safely in the forests and southern lands far from the current fighting they would still ultimately be conquered by this foul plague which now visits us."

"No!" Seren exclaimed. "Do not speak this way! We have to have hope! There has to be hope! You have the key. We can go back to a time before this whole mess began and win battles with better strategy. Something! Anything!"

"I wish it could work that way. I am sorry but it is not a device for altering time."

"But Robert! You were able to send him back to within seconds of his leaving his world..."

"Yes, but that is from one *place* to another. The past has already happened here. It cannot be revisited. The portal key only works like an elastic strap. The point of time you leave one place is as far back as it can go."

"Well at least let me go find Robert and bring back help."

Samuel touched Seren on the hand. "No dear. It is far too late I am afraid. Robert's world is far too different from ours. The people, the technology, they would not understand. Any help you would bring may pollute our world far worse than letting it be destroyed by one who had a hand in creating it."

"So you're just going to let everyone die! I can't believe that. I won't!"

"Seren, it is over. The time of man in Gwerinatha is history. If I truly believed that you could bring back help I would allow it. But there is nothing that can be done. The portal key only stays open for a short time. It opens up only large enough for a few people to get through. Even if you could go get help what would a few people do to aid us against an ever growing army?"

Seren fought back tears. She wanted to convince Samuel that he was wrong. She had now idea where to start. He was after all more than three hundred and fifty years older than her. She wondered how you can convince some one with that much age and experience anything. She grabbed his wrist and gave it one last attempt. "Samuel, I can get help I know it! Please let me try."

"Dear sweet child. I wish that you could. But you would only put to death those you brought with you. All is lost here. All is lost."

She began to cry and clench her fists. She pulled her fist up to her mouth and bit down on it trying hard to stop the tears. "You will come with me, right Samuel?"

"You know I cannot child. My place is here with my people. My fate is tied with the descendants of those I brought here. I will warn as many as I can of the impending doom and we shall face our end with dignity.

She looked over at Gefell and began crying even harder. "What of Gefell? Could he at least come with me?"

"I'm not sure I like how you added the 'at least' part when considering me." Gefell's left mouth objected.

Seren hugged him and cried even more. "I'm sorry Gefell. You know that's not what I meant."

"I'm not so sure I want to go anyway." Gefell's right mouth added.

"Gefell stays with me Seren." Samuel said sternly. "Do not worry about him. He will be more than safe. Gule's objective does not include harming non human creatures. I would assume all of the forest creatures will be safe as well. Perhaps Gefell and others like Louie would even be able to hide some of us humans there for a time. That is the only hope that I have child."

The ground began to rumble and shake again. They all looked to the ground and then at each other. The cave walls began turning slowly around them as if it were a glass jar on a table. And then the floor moved up a few inches and abruptly stopped.

"We have not much time sweet Seren. Please listen closely to my instructions. I want you to go find Robert. He will keep you safe and be able to assimilate you into his world." He gently lifted her chin up with his hand and stared lovingly into her eyes. "I do not want you to look back. Promise me you will not look back Seren. This is a new beginning for you. I know it will be very difficult. But you have a friend who can comfort you there. I feel confident that I am sending you into a safe place."

Samuel began explaining in detail the instructions of how the portal key worked. He showed her as best he could in the short time remaining exactly what she needed to know and once he felt confident she fully understood he asked her to destroy the key once she was safely in Robert's world. The cave floor rumbled again and then lifted them up and around until they were exactly where they were when they crawled into it. Samuel had set the coordinates on the portal key to the exact place that Robert had entered. He then focused the key toward the opening of the cave and the Unfinished Lands in front of them seemed to disappear as another strange world took its place. Seren gave Gefell a tearful hug and then quickly grabbed the key from Samuel. She kissed him on the cheek, turned to stare at the new opening and closed her eyes tightly. Ever since she met Robert, a boy from another world, she had dreamed of seeing America. She could listen for hours to all the stories Robert had told her of this place and now she was finally going. It didn't seem real. It didn't seem right. Her dream was coming true but the cost was enduring the worst nightmare she could ever imagine. She opened her eyes and without looking back she crawled thought the portal opening into another world.

About the Author

Brad Parnell was born in the mid-'60s into a quasi-nuclear family. He became interested the comic books handed down by older brothers, he began copying the art and drawing things out of his head. Receiving top marks in every drawing class from first grade to college, he decided to follow the path of art wherever it led.

Bored by mundane opportunities in the business world, he sought out work to stimulate his creative side. Fortunately, those in the science fiction and fantasy worlds liked his work well enough to give him the occasional illustration jobs.

Besides creating artwork, he's written some self-published comic books and his own comic strip, *Nuthouse*. Now at an a age where he can sit still for a bit longer, he has finally been able to write a fantasy novel with hopes of more to follow.

He lives with his wife of twenty years in their hometown of Louisville, Kentucky. Although currently just the two of them, they have been blessed with some wonderful cats over the years and hope to be able to open up to a new life to join them soon. Like many fellow Louisvillians he is totally caught up in college basketball and an avid U of L fan. He is a science fiction fan who loves *Star Wars*, *Lost in Space*, *Battlestar Galactica* (the original), and *Smallville*.

He is also a Beatle-maniac who was inspired to pick up the bass guitar by listening to Paul McCartney – his all-time favorite musician/songwriter.

Also from BlackWyrm...

by Ian Harac

One FBI agent
One geekette
One dead munchkin
Parallel worlds galore
An interdimensional conspiracy.
When Matt Anders stumbles across the body of a dead munchkin in a suspect's apartment, a conspiracy begins to unravel that leads him on a reality-jumping adventure to the magical Land of Oz... and beyond!
[Snarky SciFi Thriller, ages 14+]

The Veil

by Selina Fugate

A teenaged girl, Grace, draws the attention of an insane warlock. On the edge of death in a terrible accident, she makes a deal with Kracious, and is sucked into the warlock's sadistic game.
She meets a white witch that sets out to break her curse, but Kracious steps up the cat-and-mouse game with Grace's life to a new level.
Grace is suddenly shown the world behind "The Veil." A world with faeries, fallen angels, talking cats, and werewolves. A world she couldn't even imagine existed.
[Teen Fantasy Horror, ages 12+]

Albrim's Curse

by Trevis Powell

All young Albrim wanted to be was a master bowman like his father. Then a savage attack on his home cost him his family, his arm, and his humanity – all at once! Crippled and contaminated by the Curse, his beloved Gran leaves him in the care of Mute, a giant warrior dedicated to protecting humanity from the depredations of the Quarg. Albrim does what he can to assist his master and redeem himself. But can a werewolf ever really recapture his humanity?

[Epic Werewolf Fantasy, ages 14+]

Gran's Secret

by Trevis Powell

Her son is dead; her grandson Cursed. Gran has to send him into hiding to protect him, and to protect others from him. But there are those who hunt Weres to use for their own evil purposes, and they are backed by the resources of kingdoms.

When these hunters begin snooping around Gran's village, there's nothing a sweet old lady can do to protect her grandson from such people, is there?

Apparently, you don't know Gran.

[Epic Werewolf Fantasy, ages 14+]

SUGARLAND MELTING

by Sam Neace

An elderly millionaire named RJ Rockhouse opens a trailer park in eastern Kentucky, where he allows the tenants to live rent free, but the park isn't what it seems. Rockhouse is set to turn 100 years old, a sacred date for necromancers, which will allow him to transfer the spirits of himself and his wife into other bodies. Sugarland Melting is a passionate story of lost love, lost souls, betrayal, magic, and tragedy, with many surprises that will leave readers spellbound.
[Urban Fantasy, ages 14+]

IMMORTAL BETRAYAL

by Paul Lewis

Darien, viking and explorer, braves the treacherous seas to discover new lands. That changes when he falls in love. But his world is shattered when he learns she has already been promised her to another. Darien's loyalty is put to the test as he battles vampires and werewolves. Darien finds himself having to choose between the woman he loves and his very soul. With tragic romance, heart stopping thrills, and plot twists, *Immortal Betrayal* aims to please.
[Tragic Fantasy Horror, ages 14+]